COMBUSTION

ELIA WINTERS

CECAELIA PRESS

Edited by Christa Desir and Manu Velasco

Cover Design by Erin Dameron-Hill, EDH Professionals

eISBN: 978-1-951589-02-8

Print ISBN: 978-1-951589-03-5

First Edition May 2015

Second Edition February 2021

For my fellow enthusiastic product testers

1

Astrid Bailey was so absorbed in her work that she didn't hear the canister arrive. Under the golden light of a gas lamp, she bent over her cluttered work space, with its piles of gears, springs, and hand tools. She touched the switch on her new device with a hesitant nudge and watched the tiny motor whir to life. It wasn't until she set her spanner aside that she even noticed the canister resting at the bottom of the glass delivery tube, gleaming in the lamplight. How long had it been sitting there?

The note inside was written on crisp parchment with neatly scalloped edges, the stationery of a woman who valued artfulness—Becky Peregol, a woman much more ladylike than Astrid. Astrid skimmed the letter, which confirmed that Becky would be sending over a friend that afternoon for some important pre-marital education and, perhaps, a purchase. Helping young women learn their way to pleasure was one of the many duties Astrid undertook as an inventor and purveyor of felicitation devices. She'd been worried that attending the Tea and Talk women's business committee would be a waste of time, imagining a bunch of uptight prim ladies who couldn't find a climax with two hands and a gas lamp, but she had to admit she'd been wrong and was even getting a potential client out of one of her new connections there.

Astrid reached the end of the letter. Lilly, Becky's friend, would be at Astrid's flat shortly after four. Damn. She had very little time left to make herself and her flat presentable. She tossed the letter aside.

How could she make such a mess in such a small space? The front sitting room was fairly neat, the maroon velvet armchairs and sofa fortunately free of debris, but she almost couldn't see the tea table between them beneath a layer of machinery parts. After clearing off that space, she turned her attention to the display case on the opposite wall, now coated with a thin veneer of dust. It had been too long since she'd had a customer. She wiped it down with a rag stained with only a bit of engine grease, revealing the shelves of products within. The dining room table was invisible beneath stacks of bills, blueprints, and diagrams.

Finally, the front of the flat was presentable. As for the rest... She wrinkled her nose at the mess in the back. A combination of kitchen and work space, the back half of her flat was nearly indistinguishable from a garage. Racks of tools, gears, sprockets, springs, and half-finished products covered all available surfaces, including the kitchen counters. It required more cleanup than she was willing to do, but that's why she had bought those tall paper screens. A few minutes later, the messy part of the flat was hidden from view.

Astrid had barely enough time before Lilly arrived to tame her short, wild hair, wash the grease from her face and hands, and change out of her grubby workman's wear into clothing more befitting a lady. She had just put a teakettle on to boil when the doorbell chimed.

The timid-looking young woman standing in the dimly lit corridor could only be Lilly. Astrid was unprepared for how young she looked, even though she was definitely of age. Her long, blond curls were tied back with a ribbon at the nape of her neck, and her light-blue dress only added to her innocent appearance. She blinked at Astrid with a blush darkening her peach skin and an uncertain expression on her face.

"Is this the right apartment?" The paper in her white-gloved hand bore scalloped edges and Becky's distinctive handwriting.

Astrid took the young woman's trembling hand. "I'm Astrid Bailey. Do come in." The young woman hesitated before stepping over the threshold with a weak, timorous smile.

"Becky said you would be expecting me. I'm Lilly Chaffinch." She looked around at the apartment. "I hope I'm not interrupting anything. I've never done anything like this before."

"Don't worry. It's all right to be nervous." Astrid gestured to the sofa. "Make yourself comfortable. I just put some water on for tea."

Lilly's eyes never stopped moving over the contents of the flat, and Astrid knew what she must be thinking. Though the Revolution had given women the right to live alone, own property, and start businesses, it was rare to find one doing so. Even with her flat clean, Astrid's profession was clearly on display—the walls were decorated with drawings of machinery, the intricate interplay of cogs and pistons diagrammed and hung on all available spaces, except for where the large display case hung on the wall above the dining room table. Astrid could see Lilly's gaze linger on the contents therein, unspoken questions on her lips, before she finally sat on the worn velvet sofa. She rested her hands on her knees as she continued to look around, her prim white gloves worrying the light cotton fabric of her dress as Astrid went to retrieve the whistling kettle.

"How do you know Becky?" Astrid returned from behind the paper screen and set the laden tea tray down on the table.

"We were apprenticed to the same seamstress. I started there right when I turned sixteen, and she had already been there for a while. We stayed friends even after our apprentice-ships finished." Lilly had removed her gloves by this point, and the hand that took her teacup was delicate and carefully manicured. These were hands that had likely never built anything from scratch. Astrid looked down at her own. At least they were clean, and she couldn't say anything more favorable than that.

Lilly sipped her tea and set the cup carefully down in its saucer. "This is lovely, thank you." Her hands weren't trembling anymore, and she actually made eye contact with Astrid. "Becky described you, but I must admit I didn't know what to expect. She's much wiser in these areas than I am." Blushing, she looked back down at the teacup and saucer cradled in her lap. "I thought you would be much older. I'm glad you're not."

"I'm twenty-four." It seemed so old when she said it that way. "How old are you, Lilly?"

"I'm nineteen. Just this past March."

"Why did Becky say you should come here?" Astrid thought she knew, but it was better to hear it straight from

Lilly. The girl's shyness was endearing, yet it was possible she had no idea what to expect.

"I'm getting married next month."

"Congratulations."

Lilly looked up at Astrid again, her eyes wide. "I know my husband is going to expect things of me, and I'm prepared for that. But Becky said..." Lilly dropped her gaze again. "Becky said that I should enjoy those things too. She said that in these modern times, a woman should be... How did she put it? Oh, 'an equal partner in pleasure.'" She flushed pink again and focused intently on her tea. "Becky said you could teach me and that I could purchase something from you to help me."

Astrid nodded. "Becky's right. I'm an inventor. I have an entire line of products for just such a purpose."

"What kind of products?" Lilly's gaze traveled automatically to the display case across the room.

"I'll show you after we finish our tea." She would need to put the girl at ease. "Tell me about your fiancé."

Lilly immediately relaxed, beaming. "Harold is wonderful. He works in my father's bank. We've been engaged for almost a year now, and the wedding is coming up so quickly. He stood to come into some inheritance, you see, and wanted to wait until the paperwork cleared. Now that's all taken care of, and we'll be wed on the twelfth of May." A note of anxiety returned to her voice. "I do hope I'll be a good wife."

"I'm sure you'll be wonderful." Astrid had already assessed Lilly, who seemed to be the sort of quiet, dutiful, mousy girl well-suited to marriage. There was a certain endearing charm about her, an innocence that Astrid would have envied if it weren't for her unfortunate sexual naïveté. It was a good thing

Becky had recommended her. Even dutiful, mousy girls deserved satisfaction.

After tea, when their conversation lagged and Lilly's lingering gaze fell once more on the display case across the room, Astrid finally got to her feet.

"All right. Let's take a look."

Lilly let out a little gasp when Astrid pushed the button on the case, which opened up like a tray, the shelves sliding out and down, one after another, revealing a tiered array of her finest inventions. The display case mechanism was simple enough compared to Astrid's usual creations, but it always impressed clients.

Lilly stared at the wooden and brass devices, clearly confused and yet intrigued. She reached out to touch one then drew back. "What do they do?"

"They do different things. I'm going to select one for you and show you how to find your own pleasure."

"How will you do that?" Lilly looked to Astrid with wide blue eyes.

This part was always a bit uncertain. Sometimes they reacted poorly and rushed from the apartment in embarrassment or confusion, but usually they stayed.

"I'll touch you, above your clothes and below, and teach you what to do for yourself and your husband. You can have me stop at any time, and I'll stop. All right?"

If Lilly's blush had been deep before, she was positively scarlet now, understanding beginning to blossom. Her pupils dilated a bit, and she licked her lips. Astrid knew immediately that she wouldn't run. "All right."

Astrid patted her on the shoulder. "Go lie down on the sofa."

Astrid selected a device from the shelves, a small brass cylinder about as long and wide as a finger, the most basic model of her collection. This would be a perfect starter for Lilly. The young woman was lying down with her hands folded primly across her stomach, biting her bottom lip. Astrid sat on the edge of the sofa beside her and set the device on her lap. "I'm going to touch you, over your clothes. Is that all right?"

Lilly nodded, a bit more quickly this time. Astrid ran her fingertips down Lilly's neck and shoulders then cupped her breasts through the fabric of her dress. Lilly inhaled sharply and then sighed as Astrid began rubbing her nipples. Astrid envied Lilly at that moment for the unexpected sensations she was feeling for the first time. "Relax. I'm not going to hurt you. I'll stop if you want me to stop."

When Astrid began rolling her nipples between her fingers, Lilly let out a soft moan, her eyes closing. "D-don't stop." That was the response Astrid was hoping for. Astrid began inching the material of Lilly's dress upward, her other hand continuing to move from one nipple to the other over the soft cotton of Lilly's dress.

Lilly was panting when Astrid took her hands away, and she took a moment to blink her eyes open. "Is that...is that it?"

The poor, sweet girl. "No, but I wanted to prepare you. I'm going to touch you below your skirts. All right?"

Lilly nodded, expression eager.

Astrid at last slipped her hand down below Lilly's skirts and touched her at the juncture of her thighs, fingers gliding through the tight curls. This was the other moment where they sometimes tensed up, sat up, stopped her, but Lilly's legs fell out to each side, her hips arching as Astrid found the tiny nub between her legs. Wet already. This one was easy.

Astrid turned on the small brass device, pressing the button on the bottom that made it whir quietly into life, vibrating all along its cold metal length, which she tried to warm by hand. Lilly's eyes flew open at the first touch of the cold brass to her cleft.

"Wha—" she began, arching involuntarily, grasping the fabric of her own skirt.

Astrid brushed Lilly's hair back from her forehead. "It's all right. Just breathe."

Lilly settled back, still wild-eyed, and Astrid began moving the vibrator in small circles on her clit.

"What...? What...?" The woman tried to speak, her chest heaving, but couldn't finish her sentences. Astrid didn't answer, knowing words would do no good.

Lilly moaned as Astrid began circling the device a bit faster. Astrid was fascinated by this process, watching her clients come undone with gentle ministrations and a little mechanical help.

"I don't... I don't..." Lilly balled her hands tightly in the fabric of her skirt, her hips moving of their own accord.

"I promise, it keeps getting better." Astrid paused, moving the vibrator away. "Are you all right for me to continue?"

Lilly nodded and arched her hips up, seeking the contact again, so Astrid obliged. Lilly's blond hair had come undone from its ribbon and spread loose and wild over the pillow. With her tossing head and flushed skin, she looked quite different than when she'd first walked through the door that evening. Astrid recognized the signs in Lilly's body even if the woman herself had no idea what was happening. Lilly stiffened, her eyes flying open, her expression equal parts panic and arousal.

Head thrown back, she arched up off the sofa, crying out as she came. Astrid kept moving the device in small circles, letting her ride out the aftershocks, before at last switching it off and setting it aside.

Lilly relaxed at last, her lips parted, her forehead bathed in sweat. She smiled sheepishly at Astrid, but didn't seem to know what to say.

Astrid patted her on the hand. "Go freshen up."

When Lilly returned, Astrid handed her the now-cleaned vibrator. "That was an orgasm. A climax. You should have many of them. They're good for your health." The young woman studied the brass cylinder, flipping it over in her palm, then turned it on. When it whirred to life, she gave a start and switched it back off again. While she played with it, Astrid continued her instruction. "You don't have to use the vibrator, but it will make things easier for you and your husband. This way, you can share in his pleasure."

"I'm supposed to give this to him?" Lilly's fingers closed around the cylinder. "I don't think that Harold will know what to do."

"You need to show him, once you've practiced enough on your own. Trust me, he'll love watching you come." Astrid smiled. Men did always enjoy when women shared their climax. Too bad they seldom seemed to know how to get a girl there themselves.

Lilly looked back down at the vibrator. "How much does it cost?"

"That model costs four pounds." Astrid got to her feet. "If

you're interested in buying it, you'll need this charger. Here, I'll show you how it works."

After the transaction, Lilly held her handbag to her chest, the vibrator and its charger hidden inside. Her eyes sparkled, and with all propriety forgotten, she threw her arms around Astrid and hugged her. "Thank you so much. I'll tell Becky how wonderful you are. I'm going to recommend you to everyone."

If she actually did, Astrid might be able to pay her rent that month. She smiled. "I hope you do."

2

When her guest left, Astrid breathed a sigh of relief and splashed some cold water on her face. These sessions were always exhausting, far more work than the four pounds she earned, but usually the initial effort earned her a repeat customer. Now, though, she wanted her own pleasure, and she had no one to help her remedy the situation. She was not without resources, however.

Astrid's end table appeared innocent enough, but it also held her private collection. Sitting on the bed, she traced her fingers over each product, marveling again at these fine creations before choosing her favorite. This one was long and thick, made of smooth wood polished to a lustrous sheen. A finger-like nub of the same smooth wood protruded from the base, curling up as though beckoning her closer. The solid brass bottom of the device featured an array of dials. She folded the comforter back, revealing crisp sheets beneath, and looked across the bed at the large window.

When Astrid lay in bed, she could see the entire cityscape

through the window on her right. She loved that view, loved to look out on the city through the hovering gray mist and watch the droplets of rain run down the glass. Another woman might close the curtains as she undressed, but Astrid was not another woman. She left the blinds open as she slipped out of layers of clothing, garments pooling on the floor.

Sometimes she imagined being watched from the tenement building across the alley, some unknown occupant of a fourth-floor walk-up much like hers staring as she performed this most delicious of rituals. She thought about that very idea as she lay back, her naked skin exposed to the cool air, and slid her hands to her breasts.

In her fantasy, the man watching her would be tall and lean, darkly handsome, with deep, brooding eyes. He would watch her undress, watch her lie down, his gaze raking over her body from across the alley. Or perhaps he would be there in the room with her, leaning against the wall opposite her bed, dressed in a dark suit and gloves—oh, yes, black gloves—watching as she touched herself.

Astrid slid one hand down her stomach until she found the soft curls between her thighs, then moved lower, dipping a finger down into her folds. She was wet, of course. He would see how wet she was, would see her fingers circle that tiny bundle of nerves. Sparks of intensity made her toes curl against the sheets. With her other hand, she found the vibrator beside her.

This was the part where she sometimes covered up, not yet ready to risk being seen, the exposure too intimate. Looking out the window, though, into the empty flat across the alley and the city beyond, a fit of daring seized her and she left the covers off. She slipped the device down between her legs and slid the thick shaft inside.

The warm, firm wooden shaft filled her deeply, completely; the external nub nestled perfectly against her clit, designed to her precise specifications. With her thumb, she flicked one dial on the bottom and felt the shaft vibrate inside her. After only a moment spent savoring that sensation, she flicked the other dial, and vibrations coursed through the clit stimulator as well. God, that was incredible. Her muscles clenched around the firmness, and she closed her eyes, holding the vibrator steady and letting the pleasure build.

He would touch himself while watching her, running his hand down his hard cock, stroking himself as she writhed naked on the bed. Astrid pinched her nipples as the shaft continued to vibrate inside her, the stimulation pushing her swiftly to the edge. He would watch her like this, watch her desperation and need. He would be unable to look away. Climax rolled over her, stealing all thought in the breathless peak of sensation.

When she finally relaxed, she was sweating slightly, her skin glistening in the late-afternoon light still streaming in the window. The aftermath always left her feeling a bit ashamed, but the shame was almost pleasant, a heady mixture of post-orgasm laziness and recklessness. She left the blinds open as she cleaned up and dressed again, daring someone to look in, even though she wasn't sure what she would do if it actually happened.

Astrid brought a kerosene lamp over to her desk and pulled out her ledger. The figures inside were depressing. Her debt column far exceeded her income column, and the four pounds she inked in did little to remedy the disparity. With a sigh, she shoved the ledger aside again, disturbing a sheaf of parchment in the process. The papers fluttered to the ground.

Astrid picked up the papers and felt a pang as she looked at them more closely. When had she drawn these? A few months ago? Last year? She spread the most complete version across her desk.

Bailey's Felicitation Emporium, she had titled the diagram in large, sweeping letters—a blueprint for the shop she someday hoped to open. Astrid traced her fingers across over her drawing of the front counter and cash register, the display tables showcasing different devices, the salon where guests could lounge and drink tea, the back room where her most discerning clients could sample their new purchases. Her fingers lingered on her drawing of the spacious workroom in the back, organized with shelves of tools and parts.

Astrid scoffed at her own optimism. How would she ever afford such a shop? She knew the cost, had calculated it all, from the rent to the furniture to the little bell she would hang above her door. With her current financial situation, her shop was no more than a fantasy.

Her throat felt thick all of a sudden, and she tucked the blueprints away beneath her ledger.

3

———————

Eli Rutledge imagined many different scenarios when his cousin Edwina asked him to speak at her latest Tea and Talk committee meeting. As businesspeople themselves, the committee members would probably have questions for him about his successful shop. He was expecting some to be interested in his talk and others to just politely put up with him. He was expecting young women and middle-aged women, fashionable women and working-class women, but he wasn't expecting the woman in the black boots.

Amidst the crowd of chattering ladies, she remained silent and alert, studying him with no trace of shyness. Her dark eyes pressed on him like a touch as he looked around the room. It took all his concentration not to stare back at her, especially as she deftly brushed a few strands of hair off her forehead, drawing attention to her short, wildly tousled brown locks. Through several quick glances, he took in her entire ensemble. In addition to her black knee-high boots, she wore a skirt that barely brushed her knees, the fabric folded up into layers bunched thick at the bottom. As was fashionable with many young women at the time, she wore her black corset over her white, stiffly pleated blouse, the first few shirt buttons undone to reveal an expanse of cream-colored skin between her collarbones. Eli found himself staring, and worse, caught her gaze. She raised one eyebrow, managing to look both annoyed and amused at the same time, and he looked deliberately away at Edwina.

Sweet Edwina looked so excited that she might tremble apart. "Ladies, I am thrilled to have Eli Rutledge here with us today. As you all probably know, Mr. Rutledge is an accomplished watchmaker and purveyor of home goods, and he has a very successful business right here in the city proper. He's even a member of the London Business Council. I've invited him to speak with our group, since many of us are working to set up businesses of our own, and I thought he could give us some valuable advice. He also has news of a wonderful opportunity—"

Across the room, a hand flicked up, catching Edwina's attention. She stopped midsentence in bewilderment. The young woman in the black boots looked pointedly at Eli then back to Edwina, to whom she directed her question. "If this is a women's business group, how is it that the only person we've found to give us advice is a man?"

Eli definitely hadn't expected a hostile audience. When he'd rehearsed this speech last night, he had hoped they would be kind, not argumentative. At Edwina's "startled deer" expression, he knew he should help. "I'll answer this, Edwina." He turned his attention to the woman in the black boots. "That's a very good question, Miss…"

"…Bailey," she supplied. "Astrid Bailey. And you don't need to patronize me."

"Of course not, Miss Bailey." Her eyes were dark and intense, framed by long, thick lashes, and even with her skeptical expression, he was getting lost in them. Flustered, he focused on the spot between her eyebrows instead and tried to sound calmer than he felt. "Edwina is my cousin, and she invited me here as a representative of the London Business Council to share an opportunity with all of you. It would probably be more appropriate to invite a woman, since I do respect your women's group here, but unfortunately there are no women in the LBC." When she raised an eyebrow, he added, "A dilemma I hope to see remedied someday."

Astrid nodded, at least temporarily mollified. He still felt nonplussed, unnerved by the intensity of her stare and her hostility. Surely, he'd never met her before. Why was his presence so upsetting to her?

"Thank you, Astrid." Edwina jumped back into the conversation, her face red. "I promise you, you'll find Mr. Rutledge's news quite interesting."

Astrid's expression implied that she doubted this, but at least she had shut up. Eli looked back to the group as a whole, who mostly seemed interested and alert. Edwina nodded for him to continue. "Why don't you tell them all how you got started?"

Eli settled back in his seat, avoiding Astrid's gaze, directing his speech at the other women in the room. "My father has always been a watchmaker, and I learned my trade from him. He's owned the shop since before I was born, and I've worked there since I needed a stool to see over the counter." Most of the women smiled at this, and he relaxed somewhat. "We had a difficult time during the Revolution, like many businesses, but managed to persevere. After the

Revolution ended, I slowly took more and more responsibility for the business itself, eventually becoming sole proprietor about ten years ago. Shortly thereafter, I took my father's seat on the LBC."

A young woman with ebony skin and a pretty pink dress raised her hand to ask a question. She was lovely and had the self-assuredness many of these women business owners seemed to share. "What have been your most significant challenges as a business owner?"

Eli rubbed his neatly trimmed beard. He had prepared for this question. "The challenges have varied with the times. After the Revolution, in many ways it was like starting a whole new business. We had a very small customer base and had to build up our clientele almost from scratch. I'd say in that time period, branding our business was the biggest challenge. We needed to get our name out there any way we could. Now, we're established, but we face different challenges. Keeping up with current events, remaining cutting-edge with new technologies—that's what we're dealing with. Even as an established business, it's easy to be swept aside by innovation."

The young woman's question started a cascade of other questions from the rest of the group, which he answered as knowledgeably as he could. After all, these women needed his advice, so he had to think of them and not himself. They were far less experienced in business than he was, and his wisdom might make the difference in whether their businesses survived. It was not a responsibility he took lightly. He enjoyed the attention, their rapt gazes and thoughtful questions, all except Astrid, who was still sitting on the settee with her arms folded, a sour expression on her face. She didn't seem to realize what a gift she was disregarding.

After the questions had begun to lag, Edwina glanced at the clock and clapped her hands together. "All right, ladies. I want to make sure Mr. Rutledge has time to present his wonderful opportunity to all of you."

"Now, Edwina, it's not my opportunity. I'm presenting it on behalf of the council." Leafing through the sheaf of documents on his lap, he found the one he sought and then read directly from it. "The International Federation for Commerce and Trade hereby announces the tenth World's Fair, which will be held for the first time right here in Brittania from June third through the seventeenth. As you may know, a World's Fair is held every five years to celebrate the achievements of inventors and artisans worldwide and give them the opportunity to compete for the coveted Best in Show cash prize. In addition to category prizes, the Best in Show prize of ten thousand pounds will be awarded to the invention deemed to best embody the spirit of innovation and excellence so valued by the International Federation for Commerce and Trade."

Eli looked up from the document at the faces before him. "That's the news. Brittania is hosting the World's Fair. Every business owner is invited to purchase booth space to display their best products, and any inventor can enter the contest."

After a moment of stunned silence, the room erupted into excited babble. Through the chaos, Eli found himself searching out Astrid, looking for her reaction, wanting to win her over. Would this, finally, make her smile?

Her attention was focused on the woman next to her, the woman in the pink dress who had asked the first question. He could make out snippets of the women's conversation.

"...perfect for you, Astrid. With a booth, you could get some exposure, get more clients..."

Astrid stared past her friend, nodding and looking off into space. Her face was a mask of deep thought, brows knitted, her lip caught between her teeth. She wasn't smiling, but at least she didn't look so angry anymore.

Edwina clapped her hands again to quiet the group. "Ladies, ladies. Settle down. Mr. Rutledge, where can we get more information?"

"The IFCT has set up offices downtown in the bank building. They'll be giving out paperwork all week. The deadline for booth rental and contest applications is Friday the twelfth."

"We only have two weeks to apply?" Astrid's voice made him turn. "The twelfth is two weeks away. Less than two weeks. What will we need to apply? Do we need the product in hand, or can we just have the idea?"

Eli skimmed the document in his lap. "I'm not sure, to be honest. I only have the general overview. You'll have to ask the Fair Board." He had tried to put off thinking about the Fair as long as possible.

"Aren't you on the Fair Board?" Astrid raised an eyebrow.

"No. That would be a conflict of interest." He met her gaze. "I'm planning to be an exhibitor."

At that, her lips flicked upward in a small smile that seemed a challenge. "Well, then, I'll have to ask the Fair Board."

After the meeting had officially broken up and everyone stood around drinking tea and mingling, Eli sidled up to Astrid, who was chatting with the curly-haired woman again.

"Miss Bailey?"

She turned, her expression guarded, and gave him her hand. "Mr. Rutledge. Thank you for your fine presentation this evening."

"I'm all too happy to oblige." He bent over her hand to kiss it. Heaven help him, but she smelled good, like an intoxicating perfume mixed with…engine grease? Realizing he was lingering, he stood back up again and released her hand. Her guarded expression had been replaced with one of amusement. "Miss Bailey, what is it you do?"

"I'm an inventor."

That explained the engine grease. "What do you invent?"

The curly-haired woman next to her smiled against her teacup as she took a sip. Astrid shot her a look that seemed to be a warning. Then she turned back to Eli and waved a dismissive hand. "Oh, I invent all sorts of things. Mr. Rutledge, have you met my dear friend Mrs. Josian Bird?"

"Charmed." He kissed Josian's hand, his attention still focused on Astrid. "I imagine you're going to enter the World's Fair?"

Astrid's lips tightened slightly. "We'll see. There are a lot of variables to consider."

"Of course." Interesting. What might those variables be? "Have you ever attended a World's Fair?"

Astrid arched one delicate eyebrow. "I'm flattered that you think so highly of my station, Mr. Rutledge. Where were the last ones?" She tapped a finger to her lips. "Oh, right. St. Petersburg and New Atlantic, if I recall. No, I can't say I've had the means or the opportunity to make either of those flights." She flicked her gaze upward with a slight sigh and took a sip of her tea.

"Miss Bailey, if I said or done something to offend you, I

apologize." Her sarcasm and hostility were completely unreasonable given their circumstances. "I'm just trying to make polite conversation with an interesting woman."

Astrid blinked, then looked down into her tea before setting the cup on a nearby table. Perhaps he had taken her off her guard at last. When she met his eyes again, her gaze was resolute. "Mr. Rutledge, I don't mean to give the wrong impression. It's very kind of you to meet with us, when I'm sure there are other things you could be doing." Astrid put her shoulders back slightly, straightening. "But whether you realize it or not, you're the very reason women need groups like this." With a wave of her hand, she gestured to the other ladies gathered in the room. "You have nothing in common with us. You inherited a successful business from your father, who was already a prominent businessman, and your greatest achievement is to not yet have run it into the ground. Other people have given you everything you've ever needed. As a man, you can get a position on the Chamber of Commerce—or the Fair Board or the IFCT or the London Business Council or whatever—and know that when you talk, people will listen. And I'm very happy that you have the money to own a shop and rent a booth at the World's Fair, but to assume that everyone else can do the same demonstrates how completely clueless you are about the plight of women business owners in this city. So, no, you haven't said anything to offend me. Everything about you offends me."

The room had gone silent, and Eli stood frozen, staring down into Astrid's face, into her dark eyes, which suddenly widened as if she was just realizing the magnitude of her words. She flushed, her face and neck and collarbones turning a rosy shade of pink, and she pressed one hand to her lips before rushing from the room.

As she left, Eli watched her go with numb shock. Her words had been incredibly rude, and he couldn't help but feel stung. What shocked him the most, though, was his sudden and overwhelming urge to kiss her.

4

———

An unexpected knock at her door interrupted Astrid's light breakfast of toast and tea.

"I don't know what has gotten into you." Josian pushed past Astrid into the flat without waiting for an invitation, untying the ribbons on her purple bonnet as she went. "Honestly, Astrid. You can't go mouthing off to everyone you meet. That was Eli Rutledge last night. Eli Rutledge." She sank down onto the worn velvet sofa and placed her hat in her lap.

"I know who he was, thank you very much. And please, do come in." Astrid brought the teapot over with another cup then sat across from her friend on one of her high-backed wing chairs. "I couldn't help it. You know how I get."

"Cheeky and rude? Yes, I know very well." Josian took Astrid's proffered cup of tea. "But you need to stop running people off. You need those social connections if your business is going to survive."

Astrid snorted in derision and swallowed some toast. "I don't need social connections from Eli Rutledge. He's just another pretty businessman who thinks women need saving. I've had enough of them for a lifetime. I can make my own way." The men she'd dated came to mind, with their too-kind eyes and understanding smiles, wanting to save her from poverty and, ultimately, from independence. If she were to get help, it wouldn't be from a man.

"Are you going to rent a booth for the World's Fair?" Josian sipped her tea.

"I don't know. It's probably far beyond my price range." The World's Fair would be an incredible opportunity, but she could barely pay her rent, let alone afford to rent a booth at the most well-known event in the world. "But I'm definitely entering the contest. I'll scrape together the entry fee somehow."

"Oh, dear, I'd love to help you out. Maybe I can borrow some money from Warren."

Josian's smile was a bit too sympathetic. Of course her friend meant well, but her offer was yet another reminder that Josian had married into money. Josian's seamstress work and her affiliation with the Tea and Talk society were hobbies rather than a financial necessity. The two women may have grown up together in the same orphanage, but their lives were quite different now.

Astrid forced herself to answer calmly. The offer came from a place of love. "No, that's all right. I told you before, you can support my business through recommendations and purchases, but that's all I need." The smile felt tight on her face.

"Of course! I almost forgot. I'm not just here to scold you about your abhorrent behavior last night." Josian shook her small purple handbag. "I'm making some purchases. Eleanor from my bridge club is getting married in a few weeks. She's too shy to come here herself, but she certainly won't turn down a few gifts."

Astrid smiled, her entire mood brightening again, and she immediately went to her display case. "I can help with that."

Josian passed over a little wooden bullet vibe and hefted a larger model, the same type as the one Astrid had been using a lot lately. "What do you think of this one?"

"It's my current favorite." Astrid pointed out the features. "This dial here is for the main shaft, and this one here is for the external nub. Even better, they're variable motors." A turn of the dial made the vibrations escalate in intensity then settle back down.

"How does it work?" Josian turned it over in her hand, looking at the bottom. "Does it charge, like the others?"

"Yes. And this one runs on compressed air." Astrid pointed to a small vent on the bottom. "Don't block that, and you'll be all set."

Josian turned the dials on and back off again. "I don't know how you figure all this out. I can barely work the oscillating laundry crank." She smiled and shrugged, handing the device back to Astrid. "But I guess that's why you're selling and I'm buying. I think it's too complicated for Eleanor, but I'll definitely take one for me."

As Josian continued to peruse the selection, Astrid began wrapping up the new item, admiring the piece as she did so. All those hours painstakingly shaping the wood and polishing each product until it was as smooth as glass, applying the varnishing, assembling the delicate, tiny gear work—she was sure this design would be her most popular.

After a little nudge from Astrid, Josian eventually chose a

slender brass cylinder, the "beginner's vibrator," for Eleanor. Another piece of brown paper and string and this one was wrapped as Josian counted out the pounds from her handbag. Though the transaction finished, her friend still seemed in no hurry to leave, holding her wrapped purchases as she stared at the cabinet with a blank expression on her face.

"Was there something else you wanted to see?"

Josian shook her head, visibly coming back to herself. "I was just thinking about what a shame it is that you can't open your shop yet."

Astrid traced the outline of the end table with her fingertip, a sudden lump in her throat making speech difficult. She forced her emotions away. "Yes, well, the World's Fair prize money would go a long way toward making that happen."

"Then you'd best get right on it!" Josian flashed a bright smile at Astrid, who returned it with difficulty.

"I certainly will. Are you all packed for your trip?" Josian and her husband always spent May in their summer home.

Josian sighed. "Almost. I swear, it's such a chore, this packing. You'd think after five years of going up north, it would get easier, but it never does." She hugged Astrid close. "I'm going to miss you. Will you come up for a few days? You know you're always welcome."

It would be nice to see Josian, but a week in the same house as Warren might make Astrid go mad. "No, I think I'm going to need the time to work on my World's Fair entry."

Josian pulled back. "I'll write all the time. Write back, will you? If you're not too busy. I'll be back in time for the Fair opening, and maybe we can go together!"

"Maybe." She returned Josian's kiss on the cheek. "Take care of yourself."

After Josian left, Astrid leaned her back against the door. Usually, she felt lonely during Josian's month away, but her mind was already full of thoughts about the World's Fair. It might be nice to have the time alone. Her gaze landed on her cabinet of devices. None of those was unique enough to win the contest. If she wanted even a chance at the prize money, she would need something truly special.

She had no idea what to design.

Ever since arriving home the night before, she'd been mulling over possible ideas for new products. Nothing was right. The world of felicitation devices seemed suddenly too narrow: How could she improve on what she'd already created?

It had always been easy, in the past. She'd created every possible combination of oscillating and rotating and telescoping designs, and while she hadn't built them all—some, for instance, required parts she couldn't afford—none of them seemed quite right for this competition. If she wanted to win, she needed something unique.

Time was wasting. Astrid couldn't be delayed by ridiculous barriers like a lack of inspiration. She would go out and find inspiration.

5

———

Astrid's first stop was the bank building—headquarters for this year's World's Fair. Her enthusiasm dimmed at the sight of a queue of people stretching down out of the front door all the way to where she stood, half a block away.

The young man at the end of the queue doffed his hat when she tapped him on the shoulder.

"Excuse me, is this the queue for World's Fair paperwork?"

He nodded. "Yes, miss."

She peered past him. "It's a very long queue."

"Yes, miss."

Astrid settled in behind him to wait. He didn't seem interested in talking further, and she didn't press the conversation.

When at last she reached the front, the older gentleman sitting behind the desk extended a sheaf of papers and gestured to the pad of names in front of him. "Sign your name."

"I have some questions."

He looked up, surprised, and scratched the healthy growth of white whiskers on his cheek. "All right, miss. Ask away."

"Do I need to rent a booth to enter the contest?"

He shook his head. "No, miss. The contest entries will be handled separately."

"And is the contest open to any kind of invention?"

"Yes, miss. The winner of each category will receive a cash prize, and the winner of the entire Fair will receive the prize of ten thousand pounds." His muttonchops twitched as he spoke, as if he were chewing his words, and she was momentarily fascinated by them. His white skin was nearly as pale as those sideburns, like he was more ghost than man.

"Thank you." Then she was off, winding her way back toward the door and out into the bright, clear air, reading as she walked.

Fees were listed on the first page of the packet. Booth rental cost fifty pounds per day or five hundred pounds for the whole duration of the fair, the equivalent of more than five months' rent. She certainly wouldn't be renting a booth. But the contest entry fee was only ten pounds, and she could afford that. She skimmed the rest of the paperwork, aimlessly wandering through town. Finally, she tucked the sheaf of papers into her purse then looked around to get her bearings. She was standing in front of the tall glass windows of Rutledge Fine Crafts and Handiworks.

A wave of annoyance washed through her followed by a twinge of curiosity. She'd never actually been inside this shop. All she knew of Eli Rutledge was his reputation, and their tense meeting the previous night had been less than illuminating. It was hard not to feel jealous in front of those broad glass windows with their finely painted golden letters; this store was the manifestation of all her goals and dreams. He had even hung a sign in the window: *Rutledge Fine Crafts and Handiworks: As Appearing in This Year's World's Fair!*

She should probably keep going, but she was already turning the handle and walking inside.

6

<hr>

When the bell rang above the door, Eli didn't look up at first. He loved helping customers, but it was always difficult to set aside whatever task he was working on—in this case, replacing two tiny gears in a malfunctioning pocket watch. Not until he had clicked the last piece into place did he look up, and by that point, his customer had turned her back to him to examine a display table.

It took almost a minute to recognize her. For one, she'd dressed more conservatively, her plain brown skirt brushing her ankles, but her short, tousled brown hair was so distinctive that he looked closer. And when she turned, her profile came into view. Eli's fingers fumbled on the pocket watch he was still holding, and both small gears popped out of place, rolling across the countertop and disappearing into a crack in the floorboard. Astrid Bailey was in his shop.

Was she avoiding eye contact deliberately, or was she so interested in his watches that she hadn't noticed him? Leaving the broken watch where it lay, he walked over to her. He had just about reached her shoulder when she looked up, her face immediately coloring.

Her hand was small and warm when he took it in his, and upon him kissing it, her fingers tightened slightly. What could he make of that? He didn't release her hand right away, enjoying the flush that had now crept down across her collarbones. "Miss Astrid Bailey. A pleasure to have you in my shop." He probably should have stopped there, as propriety required, but had to add, "Especially since everything about me offends you."

He was rewarded by the deepening of her blush and her averted eyes. "Ah. Yes." She tugged her fingers from his. "I should apologize, Mr. Rutledge. I've been told I sometimes speak without thinking." That wasn't exactly an apology, though, and when she met his eyes again, she didn't look altogether contrite.

"Is that what brings you into my shop today? Apologizing for your reprehensible manners last night?" When her gaze hardened, he smiled. Here, in his domain, it was fun to tease her. "I kid, of course. Regardless, I'm surprised to see you here."

"Yes, well, I was out in the neighborhood, and I decided to stop in and see the competition." Her thin smile hinted at untold secrets.

Eli raised his eyebrows. "I'm competition? If I recall correctly, you were somewhat evasive about your own inventions last night."

With a shrug, Astrid looked back down at the display of watches, running her fingers across the black velvet tablecloth. "It's nothing that would concern you. I sell products primarily for women."

He took her hand off the tablecloth and examined it. "But you're not just an inventor. You're a machinist."

Her surprise was unmistakable, and she looked down at their joined hands. "How did you know that?"

"Your hand has a slight and wonderful aroma of engine grease, and there's a tiny bit under this fingernail."

For the second time in a few minutes, she drew her hand out of his again. She seemed confused about what to do with her hands, and eventually folded her arms.

The mystery of her business intrigued Eli. "You invent machines for women? Like home goods?" He glanced at the back of his shop, where he displayed his own selection of handiworks and home goods. This would explain why she saw him as a competitor.

Astrid raised one eyebrow. "Do you think we never get out of the kitchen?"

"What other kind of machines for women are there?"

Looking skyward, she shook her head. "Never mind. You wouldn't understand."

His sudden frustration stemmed less from not knowing and more from the fact that she wouldn't tell him. "Where's your shop?"

"I work from my flat. You know, on contract."

Eli leaned against the wall and thrust his hands into his pockets. "I have to confess, Miss Astrid Bailey, I'm intrigued. I've never met a woman machinist."

"Well, you can't say that anymore. You know one now." Her cheeky grin challenged him.

"And a lovely one, at that." Perhaps he was being too forward, but he couldn't mistake the chemistry between them.

He enjoyed this sort of harmless flirtation, as long as it didn't get out of hand.

She blinked, clearly nonplussed, and picked up a watch off the table to look it over. "I see you have your little World's Fair sign up in the window. That must be nice."

Not that he'd wanted to hang up the sign, of course, but he had a reputation to protect. Everyone was expecting his entry. Rutledge Fine Crafts and Handiworks had always entered the World's Fair. "Have you made up your mind about entering? Finished considering those variables?"

"I didn't realize you were taking notes on our conversation last night." Astrid set the watch carefully back on the table. "But yes, if you must know, I just picked up the paperwork. Ten thousand pounds is a lot of prize money to turn down."

"Do you think you have a chance at winning?"

Maybe that came out more skeptical than he intended. She pressed her lips together. "As much of a chance as anyone. Maybe more. I happen to have a very good idea."

"And what would that be?"

Astrid raised both eyebrows, lips twitching upward. "You're persistent, I'll give you that. I hope you don't think I'm going to tell you my winning idea."

He smiled back. "It was worth a try."

The bell over the door chimed again, and both looked up as an older couple came into the shop.

"I'll let you get back to work while I look around." Astrid slipped past him, her arm barely brushing his, and he had no choice but to leave her and assist his latest customers.

While they were examining a pair of watches, Eli leaned on the front counter again and watched Astrid. Even in the more conservative outfit, she looked fantastic. He loved the way that leather corset laced up, pressing her breasts up and out, their tops barely visible above the neckline of her blouse. When she turned away, her hips shifted beneath her gathered skirt. Even without trying, she was incredibly sexy. Did she know how alluring she was?

Astrid lingered for a while in the housewares section, staring at an automated back massager, one of his bestselling creations. The device was constructed like a chair with an open back. Large, round wooden balls on short pistons moved back and forth, spaced evenly along the open frame of the chair, where they would massage the back of whoever sat there. The machine was running, each piece moving in concert with the others.

The elderly couple was still deciding between the two watches, so he strolled back to Astrid. "You can try it, if you like."

She jumped, turning away from the machine, her face coloring. She smiled a naughty smile that brought a dozen improprieties into his thoughts. "No, thank you. It's quite intriguing, though." She glanced toward the machine once more before shoving her hand into his for a quick handshake. "I'll be going now. It was a pleasure to see you again, Mr. Rutledge."

Why the sudden haste? "The pleasure was all mine." The polite thing to do would be to shake her hand, but he couldn't resist kissing it again, his lips lingering a moment longer than was proper.

Then she was gone, almost running from the shop. He had missed something, and he didn't know what it was.

7

———

Astrid practically ran back to her apartment, too excited to think straight. Of course! The idea had come to her while studying that ridiculous back massager. Why would her clients need to handle pleasure themselves if there were some kind of chair that did it for them? This was brilliant. Now she knew what she was designing, although it made her cheeks heat to consider it. A fucking machine. She was going to win the World's Fair with a fucking machine.

Back in her flat, design ideas running through her mind, she scrabbled for sketch paper. Starting with the idea of the back massager, she first sketched out a chair with attachments. She worked on that idea for a while, figuring out where the parts would attach, what the structure would look like. When her sketch was mostly finished, she tried to look at it objectively. Ugh. Far too complicated, and also kind of frightening. Scrap that. She pulled over a new sheet of paper.

If the woman were on her back, she could set up some kind of piston to move the shaft...but that would negate clitoral stimulation, so that was no good. Perhaps a frame she could position herself against? After roughing in the outlines, she didn't like it. Too clunky, too inelegant.

Her third idea was a saddle of sorts. The woman could sit atop it. She tapped her pencil against her lips. Yes, that might work. Mind already racing ahead, she sketched as quickly as she could, adding more detail. Captivated by the concept, she pulled over another sheet of paper and began designing individual components, imagining the gear work and levers needed to put this whole machine together.

When the lines began crossing in her vision, she checked the time. Damn. Almost midnight, and she hadn't even stopped for dinner. The next day would be busy—she'd crafted a few devices to drop off with clients, and her errands would likely take her all over town. She set her papers aside to fix a snack before bed.

In bed, though, sleep refused to come, and it took several minutes to identify the sensation. While excited by her idea, it wasn't enough to keep her awake, not when she was this tired. Not until her thoughts drifted back to the handsome and presumptuous Eli Rutledge did she realize the problem.

Aroused by Eli Rutledge, of all people? The quintessential businessman, all propriety and housewares? Ridiculous. Astrid had enjoyed her share of sexual partners, but they were all casual dalliances, and none had begun with the hostility she'd felt toward Eli Rutledge.

That hostility had mostly faded, however, leaving emotions behind that were difficult to identify. He was arrogant, certainly, and seemed quite sure that a woman's place was in the kitchen; he was raised in privilege and had likely earned none of it; he would probably look down on her for being working class. In the store, though, she had definitely caught him staring at her backside. The times were changing, but most men got to know her before trying to undress her with their eyes.

Yet despite his arrogance, he wasn't hard to look at. His dark, curly hair matched his deep, dark eyes, and he had the tall, lean build she liked to imagine without that suit. His hands were strong and precise. A watchmaker's hands, strong and deft, with nimble fingers to tweak a nipple, or stroke her clit, or slide deep into her sex.

She closed her eyes. No felicitation devices needed, that night, just her fingers and her fantasy. There was no harm in this purely physical response. She'd think of him and not feel guilty at all.

8

————

The queue at the World's Fair headquarters had not gone down at all since Astrid's last visit, and she had to wait for over an hour beneath her umbrella as the drizzling rain soaked the pavement around her. As the queue dragged on, she checked her watch every few moments, hoping the office wasn't going to close before she made it to the front. When she finally got inside the building, the older man with the pallid skin and muttonchop sideburns was sitting behind the table again. For all she knew, he might never have left.

"I have my paperwork." The chill of the damp day disappeared in the excitement of this moment. Her umbrella dripped steadily onto the hardwood floor. She clutched the envelope of paperwork to her chest, her gateway into the World's Fair.

"Excellent." The man slid a paper in front of him and dipped his ink pen, preparing to add her information to the long list of names and addresses. "And what organization will you be representing?"

She hesitated. "I… Well, I'm self-employed. I work out of my home on contract."

He looked up. "So you don't have a shop?"

"I need a shop?"

Sideburn Man set down his pen onto the blotter and folded his meaty hands. "Miss, the World's Fair isn't open to just anyone." His tone indicated he was explaining the most obvious fact to a child. "You need to either represent an established business or be endorsed by a prominent businessman. Do you meet either of those conditions?"

Astrid felt as though she were looking down at herself, a detached observer watching her dreams fall apart. She struggled to keep her voice steady. She would not cry in front of this man. "No."

"I'm sorry, miss." He gave her what was probably intended to be a kind smile but instead looked forced and disinterested.

Maybe all hope was not yet lost. "Is there someone else with whom I can speak about this?" The effort to keep her voice from trembling was nearly more than she could bear.

He shook his head. "I'm the Fair coordinator. It all stops with me."

Astrid stared down at him for a long moment, not sure what to do, her feet rooted to the spot. At last, the man leaned to one side and called past her, "Next?"

Astrid couldn't remember stepping out into the street, but she found herself there, still clutching the envelope to her chest as the drizzle and fog dampened her skin and clothes. Despite the chill, she let the umbrella hang beside her, preferring the cold as a distraction to her pain and frustration. The light rain hid the tears she couldn't hold at bay.

She didn't want to go home yet. She couldn't bear to sit

and stare at her designs, so she tucked the damp envelope into her bag and continued walking through the streets. Her clothes grew wet then soaked, but the discomfort registered only dimly. The rain eventually let up and the streetlights turned on, illuminating dim circles on the wet sidewalk in the gathering dusk, and she stepped beneath an overhang to think.

Self-pity was not an emotion she liked to entertain. She hadn't cried when she'd gone into the orphanage, and she hadn't lingered on the disappointment when her first romance turned to naught. She hadn't wept or wallowed over the various men she'd taken to her bed over the years, nor slumped into sadness when her bills went unpaid or she went to bed hungry. Instead, she had learned how to survive. Over the years, she had learned that a first no was not always a *final* no. Standing under that overhang in the gathering dusk, she considered her options. The Fair coordinator had said that if she didn't have a shop of her own, she could be endorsed by a prominent businessman.

Her mind went immediately to the one person she knew who was entering the Fair, the thought accompanied by a twist of annoyance, jealousy, and some deeper emotion she didn't want to name. The thought of working with him rankled. Maybe she wouldn't need his endorsement, though. Maybe he knew a loophole from his work with the London Business Council. At the very least, she should talk to him.

Stepping out from beneath the overhang, she headed with a resolute step toward Rutledge Fine Crafts and Handiworks.

9

The evening was slow, and Eli had been fiddling with the same alarm clock for over an hour without any real focus. When the bell above the door dinged an arrival, he looked up in surprise, and at the sight of the person standing there, his surprise only increased.

"Miss Bailey?" He set the alarm clock aside. "What brings you here on a night like this?"

Astrid looked as if she'd been walking in the rain for hours. Her hair lay flat against her scalp and forehead, her coat clinging wetly to her curves. An umbrella hung by her side, seemingly unopened, and her cheeks were flushed from cold. She didn't move from her position in front of the door, so he took her hands and brought her into the shop to stand by the iron stove heating the space. "You're soaked through. You know what this umbrella is for, right?"

Astrid set both bag and umbrella down on the table nearby, turning to the stove to warm her hands. "Very funny. It hasn't been an easy day."

Her eyes looked slightly puffy, as if she'd been crying. An unfamiliar emotion sparked in his breast, making his heart twist. He clenched his fists against the sudden, ineffable urge to take her into his arms and comfort her properly. "What's upsetting you?"

Either she didn't hear him or she ignored him, rubbing her hands together in front of the stove.

Eli brought up two chairs in the back, and they sat together in front of the stove for a few minutes in silence. As the moments passed, he began to feel restless. Was she ever going to tell him why she was there?

"I need to ask you something, Mr. Rutledge."

"Eli. Call me Eli."

"Eli." She turned her chair slightly to face him. Half her face was in shadow, the rest lit by the dim light of the lamps. "I suppose you should call me Astrid."

"All right, Astrid." Her name felt sweet on his lips. "What's your question?"

"How can I get into the World's Fair?"

It wasn't the question he'd expected of her, although to be fair, he wasn't sure exactly what he'd been expecting. "I'm not sure what you mean. Anyone can get the paperwork. I thought you picked yours up yesterday."

Astrid shook her head. Her lip trembled, but then she pressed her lips more firmly together and the trembling stopped. After a pause in which she seemed to be composing herself, she spoke again. "They wouldn't take my paperwork. I don't have a reputable business, and I'm not endorsed by a sponsor, so I can't enter."

What a silly regulation. "That's ridiculous. You have a

business, so you should be able to enter. Can't you get one of your clients to sponsor you?"

She gave a bitter smile.

"I don't think that will work. My clients are women. To get a sponsor, I'd have to disclose the nature of my project, and it's not something that would interest any of the businessmen in this town." She looked down at her hands. "I thought you might know some sort of loophole."

He scooted his chair a bit closer to hers and leaned forward, resting his elbows on his knees. "I don't know of one. I'm sorry."

Astrid flopped back in her chair and folded her arms across her chest with a sigh. "I hope you have great luck in the Fair. I'm sure you'll put out something very impressive."

A familiar knot of anxiety pressed in Eli's stomach. "That is what everyone expects."

"Well, bully for you."

Her rudeness startled a laugh out of him. "It's a lot of pressure. What's your idea?"

Astrid crossed her legs at the knee and settled more into the high-backed chair. "I'm not giving you my idea. The last thing I need is some upstart businessman taking all the credit for my invention."

He had to smile. "I'm not an upstart. I have an established business here."

"Then what's *your* idea? Since you're so established and all." She unfolded her arms and then began drumming her fingers on the arms of the chair. "You don't have to worry about me stealing it, since I'm apparently a nobody. So what's the brilliant invention that everyone can't wait to see?"

Eli's anxiety flared up a bit more, mixed with sheepishness. How much did she suspect? "I asked you first."

"I'm not telling you my idea." Astrid shook her head.

"But you do have one."

"Yes. I have one. Blueprints and all."

Eli sat back in his chair, counting on the shadows to hide his expression. Watching her sitting across from him, her face a complex mix of indignation and vulnerability, the urge to confide in her rose inside him. "If I tell you something, will you promise to keep it a secret?"

Astrid narrowed her eyes and tipped her head to the side for a moment. "All right."

Eli threaded his fingers together and looked down at his hands. "I don't have an idea."

"I'm sorry?" To her credit, she didn't laugh, but the amusement in her voice was unmistakable.

Repeating it was more humiliating. "I don't have an idea for the World's Fair. I took all the paperwork, and I've been hearing how excited everyone is to see my invention, after the work I put into all my clocks and housewares and everything else in this shop, but I don't have an idea for the World's Fair." He finally glanced over. "Does that make you happy?"

She pursed her lips. "It should."

"Why should my unhappiness make you happy?"

"Because I hate you!" She threw her hands up in the air with the exclamation, although her tone was one of much more exasperation than hate. "You're rich and successful, and you have a shop, and I have to get by on these little commissioned jobs that, quite frankly, pay like shit."

His jaw dropped. "You have a mouth on you, Miss Astrid Bailey."

"So I always heard."

"You shouldn't hate me. I told you an honest fact, that I don't have an idea for the World's Fair. I think that puts us on equal footing, don't you?"

"How about I send you some of my bills, and then we can be on equal footing?" she snapped. After a moment, though, the tension drained out of her shoulders, and she slumped forward. It was like seeing her for the first time.

"You're not an easy man to keep hating, but I'm going to try."

"You can suit yourself." He was smiling despite the topic of their conversation.

"It's a bit ridiculous, you know." Astrid turned her chair more to face him. "Ironic, if you will. You have the exact opposite problem as me. I have an idea and no respectability. You have the respectability and no idea."

He stared at her, stunned by realization. Of course. The idea was so obvious, he was surprised he hadn't considered it before. "We could team up."

She blanched. "What?"

"We'll work on your invention together. Your idea and my good name. If we win, we'll split the prize money."

"Whoa, wait." She jumped to her feet. "Even if I agreed to that, and I don't, because it's ludicrous, that's not a fair split. I'm providing all the inspiration, and you're only giving me an entry opportunity."

She was right. Maybe he could provide something for her that she couldn't get for herself. "I can get you a workshop. Some place other than your flat. And I'll help fund all the parts. I'll work on it with you, fifty-fifty. That's fair."

Astrid began pacing back and forth in front of the stove, brow furrowed. "Except I hate you."

Oh yes, that little detail. "Right, except that." It was possible she would rather not enter at all than partner up with him. "I think I'm your best chance here, Astrid. Unless you still want to try and get sponsored by another local business-man." There, he played his trump card. She clearly didn't want to share her idea, and sharing with him had to be better than sharing with a complete stranger. "Otherwise, your idea may be wonderful, but it's never getting into the World's Fair."

Astrid stopped right behind her chair, her nails pressing into the lush green velvet. Her brow furrowed as she seemed to weigh all her options, and a few times, he saw her gaze rake over him from head to toe. Finally, her shoulders relaxed. "I guess you have a point."

Eli stood, trying not to look too excited. "Then tell me about your invention. You have my word, I won't steal your idea."

Astrid looked away into the dim light of the lamps, her profile aglow, and began tracing her fingers across the back of the chair. "It's not that." She paused for a long time then finally spoke in a rush. "Before we agree to anything, you should know that I'm not the kind of machinist you might expect."

"All right. What kind of machinist are you?"

Astrid's expression shifted, and she gave him a hesitant, mischievous smile. She stepped around from behind the chair and walked right up to him in front of the stove. His mouth went dry as she took the lapels of his coat in her hands, drawing him even closer and looking up at him with a certain wildness in her eyes. "I'm quite...progressive."

The very tip of her tongue pressed to her top lip. Such deliciously full lips, and he desperately wanted to feel them against his. He leaned forward, only a bit, and had to catch his balance as she stepped away to rummage in her bag on the nearby table. He had to keep his composure. Astrid returned to him holding a small brass cylinder with a narrow tip, the likes of which Eli had never seen. He took the device from her and turned it over in his hand.

Perhaps it was some kind of lipstick or face paint. He held it up to the lamplight, puzzled, and finally handed it back to her. "I don't understand. This is your business?"

"Yes." And she spun a dial at the bottom of the device.

Eli jumped when the small cylinder began to hum, vibrating intensely in her hand. His mind raced, trying to put the pieces together. Then, Astrid touched the tip of the cylinder to his collarbone, right where the white collar of his shirt met the lapel of his coat.

He twitched away in reflex. "That's..." His voice trailed off as she moved the bullet back and forth along his neck, then switched to the other side. The vibrations sizzled through him, igniting his nerves, making clear thought impossible.

"Nice?" Astrid didn't look away from his eyes, her very gaze challenging him to pull back, to call her on her inappropriate behavior. Propriety be damned; he had no intention of stopping her.

"Very nice." His voice sounded breathless in his own ears. Astrid reached up to run the device along the back of his neck, wrapping her arm up and over his shoulders, bringing her body very close to his. He was losing his focus, his entire thought process swept away by her flowery smell and some very improper thoughts about what she might look like under all those clothes.

"I invented this." Astrid returned the cylinder to his collarbone, and he swallowed, feeling her gaze on the column of his throat.

Clearly, there was something he didn't comprehend, some missing piece to this puzzle. This was a neck massager of some kind, unique in design but not scandalous, no matter what his racing mind might conjure from her proximity and her touch. "I don't think I understand, Astrid."

Rather than pull away, she continued to touch him with the brass cylinder, moving it in small circles in the center of his chest, meeting his eyes with her own. Arousal ran hot through his blood, and only through supreme self-control could he keep its physical signs at bay.

Astrid looked down at the center of his chest, where she was still drawing patterns across his shirt. "I get lonely sometimes, Eli, and I like this device. I like it very much." Looking back up at him, she slid the vibrator over to one side, brushing lightly over his nipple.

Oh, holy hell. Eli jumped backward as if stung, one hand automatically moving to his chest then clenching into a fist. He wasn't going to touch his own nipple right in front of her. Astrid still wore that devious smile, and understanding clicked into place all at once. Images ran through his mind: Astrid lying on her bed, naked, that same little cylinder pressing down between her legs, her back arching in ecstasy.

No wonder she didn't tell people about her business. Machines for women, indeed.

He should think this over. A business like this brought an entirely different set of complications, and he should not get involved while his body still thrummed with heat and desire. Instead, he stepped forward again, drawn in by her magnetism and a sudden, unexpected recklessness. If she was going to play dirty, then he could be her match. As he took the device from her, her eyes widened in surprise.

He turned the still-buzzing cylinder over in his hand and watched it gleam in the lamplight. "You make these."

"And others like it. A whole range." Her gaze didn't leave his hand as he brushed his fingers over the metal.

He wanted some turnabout, to unseat her as she'd unseated him. His cock was throbbing against his pants, now, and he couldn't be bothered to worry that she'd notice. They were in unfamiliar territory, far beyond the bounds of propriety.

"I'll bet it gives lovely massages." He touched it lightly to the side of her neck, right where it joined her shoulder. Her lips parted, as if she couldn't believe what he was doing.

"It does."

Her voice definitely trembled a bit. Without breaking eye contact, he moved the cylinder down, sliding it inch by inch over her breastbone, then down the front of her corset, past each hook in the front, tracing it all the way to her skirt. How much would she let him get away with? How much did he have the nerve to try? When he brushed the juncture of her thighs through the fabric of her skirt, she grasped his lapels to steady herself, her eyes fluttering closed in a way that sent even more blood to his impossibly hard cock.

It seemed she wasn't going to stop him at all.

Before he could let himself go too far, he pulled away and switched off the vibrator, pressing it into her hand. "You have quite a naughty little product there." He turned aside, trying to steady his own breathing, pulse thundering in his veins.

When he finally glanced back at Astrid, she was blinking up at him through heavy-lidded eyes. "I have more."

He opened his mouth, ready to ask to see them, then paused as sense came flooding back. He was a respectable businessman, a member of the London Business Council, a prominent and upstanding citizen. He wasn't the kind of man who threw tradition to the wind and jumped on board with a new business venture. Ideas had to be drafted, refined, tested, proved. Astrid was unpredictable, wild, adventurous...everything he wasn't. His throat closed up.

Seeming to sense his hesitation, Astrid dropped the device back into her handbag. "So now you know why I can't ask a businessman to endorse me. Like you, they're all prudes."

"I'm not a prude." But he had decorum and decency, qualities Astrid Bailey seemed to lack, even if he couldn't help wishing he had her creativity. "But these products are scandalous. They might even be illegal. I can't be mixed up in something like that." What would the London Business Council think?

"They're not illegal." Astrid drew herself up to her full height, which was not very significant compared to him. "And the only reason they're scandalous is because the stodgy London business owners like you are still living in the last century."

Eli hesitated, rubbing his beard. This could be what ruined him, sending him into destitution as his father always feared. Was he actually going to lend his good name to an enterprise such as this?

And yet, he had no alternative. It was already May second.

The deadline to enter the World's Fair was only ten days away, and he was no closer to an idea of his own than he had been two months ago when the IFCT first green-lighted the whole endeavor. He could associate himself with Astrid's products or be branded a failure for the entire town.

She stood before him, head held high, but her shoulders trembled. She was risking a lot just by coming here. Yes, these devices were risqué, but she insisted they were legal, and she would likely know the regulations more than he did. Perhaps he could lend a bit of respectability through his endorsement. After all, his family had been business owners in London since before the Revolution, and the name of Rutledge was only associated with quality products. Plus, she was tenacious, fiery in a way he had always lacked. Her passion painfully illuminated his predictability. The partnership could be good for both of them.

"All right, I'll partner up with you."

Astrid raised an eyebrow. "You're assuming I'm going for this?"

He blinked. All that debating, and he hadn't considered she might say no. "Why wouldn't you agree? I'm a pillar of this community. You're lucky to get my endorsement." He may be predictable, but he was the kind of predictable that was the backbone of the London Business Council.

Astrid put both hands on her hips, her mouth open. "Good thing you haven't gotten a swelled head. My God, you're so full of yourself. Why should I want to share credit with you when I'm the one doing all the work? I get, what? Your name?"

"You get a workshop and supplies, and you also get an

entry into the World's Fair. Which—let's face it—you're not going to get without me." He folded his arms.

For a long moment, she stared into his eyes across the space between them, considering. Then her shoulders sagged. "Fine. But I don't much like it."

"Well, I don't much like it either, but it's probably the best we're going to get." Eli looked at her handbag on the table, the place into which she'd dropped the massager. "So I'm assuming your invention is one of those naughty devices, then?"

"It is. Not that one, though. Something entirely new."

"Are you going to tell me what it is?" She'd piqued his curiosity, and now he wanted to know the depths of this enterprise. There couldn't be that many styles of product like the one she'd shown him.

Biting her lip, she shook her head. "Not yet. You're not seeing my plans or my collection until I have your name on that paperwork. When are you free?"

"What's today, Tuesday? I'm free tomorrow. I have a shop-girl who runs the business on Wednesdays and Thursdays."

"Tomorrow morning, then. Meet me downtown at the bank building at nine, right when they open, to submit the paperwork. Once everything is official, then I'll take you back to my flat. We'll have civilized toast and tea, and I'll give you a tour of my workshop."

"And then we'll be business partners?"

She hesitated. Perhaps she was still uncomfortable with him. "Yes, then we'll be partners. Good night, Eli."

As she pulled open the door, he called after her. "Wait."

Her hand on the doorknob, she turned back; he was

already hurrying toward her. "It's late. You shouldn't be out alone. I'll call you a hansom."

He stepped out onto the street and flagged down a passing cab out of the fog. After slipping the driver a generous fare, he helped Astrid into the cab, his hand lingering on hers. "I'll see you in the morning, Astrid."

She nodded, several emotions passing over her face. "Until tomorrow, then."

10

———

Astrid waited outside the bank building for Eli, torn between wishing he would hurry up and wishing he wouldn't show at all. She was in over her head already; his behavior was unpredictable. He unsettled her. When she first pulled that little vibe out of her purse, the sample she showed prospective clients, her intent had been to see if he frightened easily. Instead, he'd been so forward, and she'd been shaken up for the rest of the evening.

His initial confusion was amusing, though. Despite her intimacies over the years, she'd never shown any of her wares to men before. Women, yes—women who were surprised and nervous and ultimately very, very happy—but never men.

She spotted Eli crossing the street, drawing his scarf a bit tighter against the early morning wind, grinning as he caught sight of her. Why did he have to be so handsome? It would be easier to continue disliking him if he didn't have those cheek-bones, those deep, dark eyes, that bright smile. He jogged up to her.

"Have you been waiting long?"

"No, not long. Are you ready?"

"Yes, let's get this taken care of." The queue was shorter at this hour of the morning, and they were soon inside the bank building. Sideburn Man was still staffing the table. Did he ever go home?

At the sight of Astrid's companion, Sideburn Man stood and took Eli's hand in both of his. "So good to see you, Mr. Rutledge. I was hoping you would turn up." His gaze fell on Astrid. "Back again, miss?"

"She's with me, Reynold." Eli extricated his hand. "Astrid Bailey, this is Reynold Halstead of the IFCT."

Reynold shook her hand, the gesture perfunctory as he never looked away from Eli.

Eli took the papers from Astrid. "We're here to turn in paperwork for the World's Fair."

"I see." Reynold adjusted his glasses and drew some paperwork toward him. "And will this be a booth registration, or is it only for the contest?"

Eli answered again. "Both." The booth would be for Eli's shop, and the contest invention would be her design.

The rest of the conversation took place between Reynold and Eli, and Astrid might as well have been invisible. The process was interesting enough to overcome her annoyance, though. Sideburn Man—Reynold—had an entirely different manner when dealing with Eli: friendly, affable, the two of them having genial conversation as equals. No matter what rights women may legally have, the true inequalities were evident in moments like this.

After Reynold had reviewed all the information and

collected Eli's cheque, he handed Eli a written confirmation of their entry. "All entries will be confidential until the Judges' Viewing on May twenty-seventh." Reynold shook Eli's hand then, after a moment's pause, Astrid's. "Best of luck to you both."

Once outside, Astrid snatched the confirmation paper out of Eli's hand, elation washing away any previous irritation. This was it. Everything was official.

"I believe we're in business." Eli turned up the collar of his greatcoat against the wind. "Now, are you finally going to show me this shop of yours?"

Astrid's flat lay just beyond the outskirts of London proper, at the edge of what could be considered a decent neighborhood. Astrid kept expecting Eli to make snarky comments about his surroundings or remind her that he was accustomed to better living arrangements, but he only looked around at the tenements and remarked that he'd never been to that part of town before.

"I imagine not. It isn't exactly the city." Her key jammed in the lock, as usual, and it took a bit of force to unstick it before she could let him in. "I'm up on the fourth floor." As they climbed the stairs, her heart quickened with more than exertion from the climb. This was the first time she'd taken a man back to her flat for any reason. Her dalliances over the years always happened at her partners' homes. Although her relationship with Eli was strictly business, the opportunity for more lingered in her mind as they climbed the stairs. He might be insufferably arrogant, but he was also strikingly handsome, and she would probably enjoy taking him to bed if she didn't try never to mix business with pleasure.

"This is it." Astrid unlocked her front door and stepped

aside. Eli crossed past her, looking around as he took off his greatcoat, revealing a high-necked button-down shirt with a vest and slacks. Closing the door behind her left them alone together in her flat, which seemed much smaller than ever before.

Eli examined a small cog from the nearest table before setting it down again. "You really are a machinist."

"Wonders never cease." She couldn't keep the sarcasm out of her voice as she put water on for tea. Did he think she'd been lying?

Eli immediately began examining the large glass display case of her wares, and a strange self-consciousness settled over Astrid. The water needed to boil so she had something else to do besides watch him examine her most intimate creations. Eventually, Eli turned away from the display case to look around the rest of the living room.

"You have a nice flat. I don't meet many women who live alone." Eli sat down on the sofa. Hopefully he wouldn't notice the worn spots in the velvet, places where the maroon fabric had faded to a dusky rose.

Astrid began setting up the cups for tea. "I'm not like most women."

"Yes, I think we covered that last night." He pointed to the display case. "So are those…?"

"Let's have tea first." Astrid stayed near the kettle, willing it to boil, not quite ready to broach that conversation yet.

"Of course." He continued to look unabashedly at the cabinet from across the room, his gaze curious and with no signs of the intimidation she'd expected.

After the kettle finally began to whistle, she brought the

tray over and sat across from him on the wing chair, handing over a cup to his murmured thanks.

Their conversation stayed on mundane topics like the weather and a bit of light politics, but when their teacups were at last set aside, Astrid couldn't delay any longer. She had his signature on the paperwork, so he couldn't run, and they might as well get on with it. She got up and flipped the switch that unfurled the display case.

"Brilliant." Eli crossed the room as the panels began folding down. He reached past her toward the display, then hesitated. "Can I pick them up?"

At her nod, he picked up a large brass cylinder, the top half of which was segmented like a caterpillar. At first, he held it as if it were fragile and could break at any moment, his touch hesitant.

"Oh, for heaven's sake." She flicked the switch. The top segments began to rotate and oscillate in a pattern, each moving after the other in a wave, so the entire top half swiveled around in a wide circle. Eli stepped back in haste, nearly dropping the product. Then he tentatively wrapped his fist around the shaft as the top half continued to spiral and press outward against his palm. His expression was unreadable. Surely this would be the moment when he blushed and stammered and got all uncomfortable. Instead, he smiled as he switched off the device and set it back on the shelf.

That secretive smile lingered as he moved on to another product, the wooden one she currently favored. This time, he showed no hesitation, flicking both dials and feeling the vibrations first with his palm and then his fingertip.

He worked his way around the case, moving to one side then to the other, and Astrid followed him, staying nearby as he investigated. When women handled her products, she always thought of the construction and effort that had gone into each device. Eli's touch, though, brought to mind lurid fantasies: his hands touching her with this same delicate care, his focused attention on her body and not just her creations. Although she'd characterized him as prudish, he examined these products with no discomfort or self-consciousness. Perhaps she'd misjudged him. The idea intrigued and unsettled her equally. Her irritation with his privilege was easier to wrangle than this chemistry between them.

Eli finally stopped when he reached the last product in the display case, one she didn't sell very often but had enjoyed designing. The contraption's mess of small straps spilled out of his grip. "How does this work?"

"Give me your hand." This invention's complexity never seemed to appeal to her clients, most of whom wanted something easier to use, but she was proud of her design as she carefully strapped it to Eli's outstretched right hand. A leather band held a small pouch of machinery to the back of his wrist, and thin cords ran from the pouch to small leather loops that slipped over each finger, each with a small brass device attached, fitting between the first and second knuckles but leaving his fingertips free.

Eli flexed his hand, turning it over. "Interesting. What does it do?"

Astrid flicked the dial on the machinery pouch. Eli jumped in surprise as his fingertips began vibrating, then he smiled. "Oh, I see." He touched his own arm then reached out and touched hers, sending a shock wave all through her senses that made her pull immediately away. "Ticklish?"

"A bit." It was easier than telling him even his most gentle touch turned her on—to her continued annoyance. He pulled away, then, and switched off the device.

"My hand feels odd now." He unfastened the straps and flexed his fingers.

"It does that." She set the device back in the case.

"How does your business work? Women come to you, and you sell them these…?"

"Felicitation devices." Astrid absentmindedly fingered a gear lever that had been left on the end table. "I build my business mostly on referrals."

Shaking his head, Eli seemed to consider his next words before speaking. "I guess I didn't know that women even knew how to use devices like these."

That was a fair assumption. "Some women don't. I teach many young women how they work and what they can be used for."

Eli's eyebrows went up, but he didn't ask for more details. Instead, he began wandering back toward her workshop, which she hadn't hidden behind paper screens. She followed close behind. "All right," he said. "Now that I've been in your flat and seen your strange devices, signed all the paperwork, and have no real way out, will you show me your invention?" He picked up one of the papers scattered across her desk, the blueprints for her future shop.

She snatched it out of his hands. "That's not it."

"Bailey's Felicitation Emporium?" He looked at the back of the paper she now clutched to her chest. "You want to open a shop?"

She must look like such an amateur to him, and she resented her flush of shame. Ducking her head, Astrid rolled up the blueprints. "Someday. Maybe. We'll see."

"That's an ambitious endeavor."

It was difficult to tell if he was making fun of her. To change the subject, she pulled the design plans from the pile. "I'll show you my invention. Come sit on the sofa."

He perched expectantly on the edge, his dark eyes looking so earnest, she couldn't help but smile, some of her earlier irritation fading.

"It doesn't have a name yet." She brought over the latest version of her design and sat next to him. Her leg pressed against his through the thin cotton of her skirt, the sudden intimacy distracting despite the inappropriate nature of all their interactions so far. Swallowing, she spread the blueprint out across both their laps.

He focused on the document, making sense of her rough sketches. "So...it's a...a..."

"A fucking machine."

His head jerked sharply toward her. "What did you call it?"

"A fucking machine." Her cheeks must be bright red, but she would *not* let this moment embarrass her. This was her business.

"Why would any woman want one of these?" He pulled a pair of wire-framed spectacles from his vest pocket and slipped them on, the gesture so sexy, she was momentarily speechless.

Struggling to regain her composure, she returned to his question. "Who would want one of these? You're kidding. A woman who doesn't have a man in her life, perhaps? Or perhaps a couple who are feeling adventurous. A man who wants to watch?"

"Or a woman who wants to be watched?" Eli locked eyes with her, and the room suddenly became much warmer. God, she didn't want to be the one to break eye contact, but his gaze burned into her like a hot coal. Fortunately, he looked back down at the design. "All right, I see. So it's some sort of chair, and she sits over it, I suppose." He traced the lines with his finger. "Like a saddle. And this here"—he tapped the illustration of the shaft, then paused, a blush rising in his cheeks—"this part moves?"

"Yes. Up and down."

Eli went silent, staring at the blueprints while rubbing his chin in thought, before exploding into speech. "My back massager! You got this idea from my back massager, didn't you?"

Astrid had to smile at his shock. "A perfect model of automated pleasure."

"You were looking for inspiration in my shop?"

She might as well admit it. "Yes. So what do you think of the machine?"

"Well, the design itself will need some tweaks, I'm sure." He studied the paper.

"Of course. It's just a preliminary model."

"But the idea...the idea is fascinating." Looking off into the distance, he seemed to imagine the finished product. Then his half smile faded. "This is going to scandalize everyone in the World's Fair. Are you sure this is legal? If this is illegal, I can't be part of it. I have standards to uphold."

"Of course it's legal. I told you, this is my business." Exasperated, she rolled up the blueprint and got up to put it back on her desk. The man probably never took a business risk in his life. She likely had endless outbursts like this ahead of her if they were going to work together.

Eli folded up his spectacles and tucked them back into his

vest pocket as she sat down next to him again. At last, he shrugged. "I suppose I'm in this until the end. You have my signature on those forms."

What a curious mixture of contradictions this man was. Astrid studied his profile. On one hand, he seemed totally comfortable with her felicitation devices, curious about the machinery. On the other hand, when it came to business, he was stodgy and uptight. The more he clung to his propriety, the more she wanted to make him lose it.

Before she could stop herself, she reached out and traced her fingertips along his arm. "Working with me might not be that bad. You might even enjoy it."

Eli met her eyes, and his gaze was open and vulnerable. Oh, Astrid wanted to kiss him, wanted to draw those lips to hers, grip his firm shoulders, and hold him against her until all his uptight propriety melted away. She swallowed. Any advances would probably be unwelcome, and she shouldn't go too far, anyway. The flirting was fine, the touches borderline but still safe. To go beyond that would distract her from the work they needed to accomplish. Her business needed to be her focus right now. She had no time for dalliances, even if a dalliance might help her dig into the series of strange contradictions that was Eli Rutledge.

"We'll have to work on this when I'm not at my shop." Eli sat back, the moment passing. "I assume you have your own responsibilities during the week."

The tension broken, a mixture of relief and disappointment settled over Astrid. "I do. Also, we'll need a space to design and build. You said you would take care of that?"

"The workshop beneath my store is in use, and I have employees who sometimes go down there. We need someplace more private. I'll rent us something." He tapped those distracting, long fingers on his thigh, thinking. "Also, I'd like to take you to dinner."

Astrid blinked. "What?"

"Dinner. You and I." He gestured between them. "A meal, in public, where we can get to know each other a little better."

He must be playing at something. "Just dinner?"

Eli tipped his head to the side. "Yes, just dinner. We're business partners now, and I don't know anything about you. Can I pick you up here tomorrow evening at seven?"

His invitation seemed innocuous, if unexpected. "All right."

He thought a moment before adding, "Also, it will be somewhere nice."

So he was worried about her embarrassing him. She narrowed her eyes, trying to rein in her sudden irritation. "I'll try to refrain from whoring myself out in public, then."

Eli's mouth opened in an O of surprise. "I didn't mean that. I just wanted you to know in case you were wondering what to wear. I'm sorry if I offended you." His concern was so sincere that Astrid felt like an arse. She couldn't get her bearings in this conversation.

"It's all right."

After gathering up his coat, Eli waited with his hand on the doorknob. "Thank you for the tea and the tour. It was very enlightening." He pressed his lips to her hand as always, lingering, and then he was gone.

For a long moment after he'd left, she stared at the closed door, heartbeat loud in her ears. She'd made a business of understanding women, learning what they wanted and how to give it to them. Men had always been straightforward—fun for sex, acceptable for companionship, but predictable and uninteresting. It had been a long time since she'd met a man who puzzled her, and the puzzle made her want him like she seldom wanted anyone.

She needed to figure out Eli Rutledge.

11
___

When the hansom cab pulled up in front of his building, it took Eli almost a full minute to realize he had arrived home. He'd been so distracted by thinking of Astrid and her felicitation devices that he continued to sit on the plush leather seat, staring at the empty bench opposite him, until the driver swung the door open and peered in. "We're here, sir."

After paying the man, Eli continued into his flat, still walking through a mental fog. He lived on the other side of the city proper, his brownstone a fair bit larger and more nicely appointed than Astrid's. No surprise, since she wasn't even a shop owner. Maybe not a shop owner, but definitely a business owner. That cheeky woman had taken his back massager and turned it into...

A fucking machine. In his mind, he heard her say it, her full lips wrapping around the words with only the slightest blush. Watching her smile, he could imagine the way she would look in the throes of climax, her composed exterior yielding to her primal, wanton instincts.

His cock throbbed against the confining fabric of his trousers. This wouldn't do. He headed into the bedroom and closed the door behind him, then drew the curtains across his large windows.

Astrid was the only thing on his mind as he unfastened the buttons on his trousers and freed his erection. For days, he had fought these fantasies, but at last he gave free rein to his basest urges. Closing his eyes, he could imagine her small, deft fingers wrapping around his cock, rather than his own hand. From there, the entire fantasy filled his mind in the space of a breath.

Astrid straddled his thighs, naked in the lamplight. His imagination filled in the curves of her body, the tight peaks of her nipples, the curls at the apex of her thighs. One deft hand squeezed his shaft while the other cupped his sac. Her touch was confident with experience, so different from the women who needed instruction and encouragement. After a few long, smooth strokes, she began to tease the head, her thumb tracing back and forth along his slit. The sensations stole his breath; a sharp rush of pleasure had him arching into his own hand. *Her hand.*

Already approaching the brink, he slowed down, wanting to savor this fantasy.

Astrid paused in her stroking, still holding him tightly, and brought her hips forward to rub his shaft against her clit. She threw her head back, closing her eyes, a moan escaping her lips. He could almost hear her. Moving her hips forward a bit more, she raised herself above him, positioning his cock then sinking down until just the head penetrated her wet folds.

The pressure of his own grip squeezing the tip of his cock

was the tightness of her sweet quim, and he groaned aloud in the empty flat.

Holding herself above him, she met his gaze and slowly sank onto his shaft.

With his other hand, Eli firmly grasped his cock, now working himself over with both hands, his breath coming in short gasps at the idea of her sheathing him in snug, wet heat.

Lifting her hips, she took him in and out an inch or two at a time then added more, each stroke faster than the last, her pussy impossibly tight. Throwing her head back, she cried out in fulfillment, muscles fluttering along the length of his shaft.

He came hard, exploding, his climax shuddering through him with an intensity that momentarily left him breathless. The aftershocks continued to rock him for moments afterward, his hands still tightly wrapped around his cock. The fantasy dissolved, and he was alone in his flat again, sticky and spent.

Guilt washed over him as he stripped off his clothes. If he wasn't careful, Astrid Bailey was going to get into his head for good.

12

———————

"Morgan's?" Astrid stared up at the imposing brick edifice of one of the nicest restaurants in all of London, glad she'd dressed conservatively that night. Her hand tightened on Eli's arm. "You're taking me to Morgan's?"

"It certainly seems that way, doesn't it?" Sweeping her across the street, one arm curved behind her back, Eli gave her no time to protest. Everyone entering the restaurant was dressed impeccably, and although she'd worn her nicest dress —a floor-length ensemble in deep purple—the sense that she didn't belong weighed on her shoulders like a heavy stole. Eli blended seamlessly with these people in his tailcoat, but Astrid would surely be thrown out of the restaurant at any moment.

Once the thought occurred to her, though, right when the maître d' began escorting them to a table, she put the idea from her mind. She had the same right as any of them to eat a delicious meal in a fancy restaurant. With that reminder, she put her head back and cast what she hoped was a dazzling smile to Eli as he pulled out her chair for her.

After ordering the special, figuring that was the safest option when she couldn't pronounce anything on the menu, she drank her wine and wondered where to begin. There were so many things she wanted to know about Eli Rutledge.

Before she could ask anything, though, he folded his hands and smiled at her across the table. "How did you get started as a machinist?"

"My mother was a machinist." The wine felt too warm her empty stomach, so she switched to her water glass.

"Your mother?" Clearly this wasn't the answer he'd expected.

"Yes, my mother." Astrid pursed her lips in irritation. "We women haven't spent our lives being seamstresses, you know."

He didn't take the bait for a fight. "What did your mother build?"

"Some of everything." Memories of her mother were hazy with time and the inaccuracies of childhood, but she could picture her mother leaning on a worktable, hair slipping out of its twist and falling across her goggles, carefully fastening screws and levers into place as little Astrid watched nearby. "She did general repairs on contract when she could find someone to hire her despite the restrictions on working women." The next part was clearest, though. "Mostly I remember her making guns."

"Guns?" Eli set his wine glass aside.

"Yes. My parents aided the Revolution." Astrid ran a finger around the top of her water glass. "My father was a writer who produced anti-government propaganda. My mother designed and manufactured guns for the Underground. We lived in hiding, moving from one place to another to keep from getting caught. It paid off in the long run, I suppose, since we won. But my parents were both killed when I was ten." After all these years, it didn't hurt to tell the story, but the sympathy in Eli's eyes was still welcome. "It's all right," she added quickly. "They died for a good cause. The Revolution made a drastic change in living conditions for the poor, so I was raised well in the orphanage. My mother had taught me a few things, and I had a natural aptitude for machinery, so I was apprenticed when I was fifteen, a full year early." She had already spoken too long, so she drank more water. "What about you? Tell me about your family."

"You already know much of it." Eli picked up the fork to examine it, pausing before telling his story. "My father started Rutledge Fine Crafts and Handiworks before I was born. I haven't yet—how did you put it?—run it into the ground, so I'm the main proprietor now." His smile showed no hard feelings. "I must confess I don't know much about the Revolution. My father took my mother and me out of London when it was deemed unsafe, and we returned when the fighting had ended. We were standard merchants, so the new regime didn't change much for us."

"You were middle-class men." Astrid couldn't keep a note of bitterness from her voice. "The Revolution helped the lower class and women. Did you know that, before the Revolution, it was illegal for my mother to work? To own property? None of the things I do now would be possible if it weren't for their sacrifice. And when tight-arsed misogynists like Reynold Halstead tell me I can't enter the World's Fair because I'm not a man..." She'd gotten louder and now forced herself to speak more quietly, looking down at the tablecloth. He must think she had no class. "I'm sorry to get carried away. I know my life is so much better after the Revolution, but it's still unfair, and that frustrates the hell out of me."

When she chanced looking up, Eli was studying her with a curious intensity, no sign of disgust in his expression. "Reynold wasn't keeping you out of the World's Fair because you're a woman. It's because you don't operate out of a storefront."

"He asked me to secure the endorsement of a business*man*. As if my business has anything at all to do with men." She started to roll her eyes then caught herself. "Present company excepted."

"How did you get involved making these felicitation devices, as you call them?" Eli rested his chin on his hand.

Astrid's cheeks heated. That wasn't a story for a fancy restaurant. "I'm monopolizing our conversation. Really, you should tell me more about yourself."

"After this." He nodded. "Go on, please."

The truth was unsavory, even for someone who cared about her reputation as little as she tried to. In the presence of the upstanding citizen Eli Rutledge, her past felt increasingly scandalous.

But he wanted the truth, so he would get the truth and maybe learn better than to ask. "All right." Entwining her fingers on the table, she leaned forward and spoke quickly and quietly. "A few years out from my apprenticeship, I was struggling financially. My five years of living credits had run out, and I couldn't pay my rent, so I found a place to stay in the Lahey Emporium."

Eli's blank stare wasn't much of a surprise. Maybe the full

name of the business would stir his understanding. "The Lahey Emporium for the Pleasurable Arts?"

A flash of recognition showed in his eyes, followed by scandalized surprise. "The brothel?"

"Yes, the brothel." Astrid returned to her wine, welcoming the heady feeling when she took a large swig. "Cecily took me in."

"So you were a...?" Eli swallowed, looking her up and down, unable to complete the sentence.

His judgment rankled, even if it wasn't surprising. "It shouldn't matter if I was." Clearly it did, though. For a moment, she wished she *had* worked at the brothel so she could shock him all the more, but she told the truth. "But no, I wasn't actually working there, not in the way you're thinking. Cecily gave me cheap lodging in exchange for some clerical help. In that environment, it was only a matter of time before I put my skills to a new type of machine, and Cecily became one of my first clients. She taught me everything I know." Astrid stopped there, not caring to elaborate to Eli on how much Cecily had taught her.

She studied his face for signs of shock, but his dilated pupils and heavy breathing indicated a different kind of interest. The undisguised hunger in his eyes made her body hot all over, and she took a sip of water to steady herself—any excuse to look away from that deep, dark gaze. She needed to put the focus back on him before this conversation led down even more dangerous paths. "Do your parents still live here in the city?"

"Hmm? Oh, right." Coming back to himself, he shifted in his chair. "No, not anymore. They live out in West Chester."

Not even the middle class could afford a house out in West

Chester, one of the last rural swatches in all of Brittania. He must be even wealthier than she thought. "I see. Do you visit them often?"

"When I can get away. I'm quite busy much of the time." He sipped from his wine.

If Astrid's parents were alive, she would visit them all the time. Of course, her parents never would have left the city, not even for some manor house out on the West Chester moors. She wanted to call him out on his unearned good fortune but just said, "West Chester. That must be nice."

"They seem to like it."

"Do you have any siblings?" If she kept asking simple questions, she could ignore any irritation.

"No, actually. Not anymore." Eli fiddled with the edge of his napkin. "I had a sister, but she got the fever. I was seven when she died."

Astrid's stomach lurched from resentment to guilt. Just a moment ago, she wanted to scold him for a life without hardship. "I'm sorry," she managed. Eli's money didn't mean he hadn't experienced his share of tragedy. "That must have been difficult."

Eli set his napkin down. "My mother took it quite hard. That's when my father first started renting the house out in West Chester. Mum couldn't be near Emily's room, so it was good for her to get out of the city. When the Revolution started, that's where we went. I grew up between the city and the moors."

For a moment, she imagined Eli as a teenager, with unruly black hair, dark eyes, and cheekbones too sharp for his face, sitting alone on the windswept moors. The pang in her heart hit suddenly, sharply, her sympathy humanizing Eli even as she tried to keep wayward emotions at bay. "I never had any siblings," she said to break the silence. "I grew close to Josian in the orphanage, though. She was a year older than me, and she took me under her wing, so to speak." Astrid smoothed her napkin over her lap. Eleven-year-old Josian had seemed so worldly and wise, teaching Astrid how to make her way in the institution, becoming the closest thing to a sister she would ever have.

"She was the woman you introduced me to at the meeting." Eli finished his wine then refilled both their glasses from the bottle on the table. "You two are still close, then?"

"I suppose. We have very different lives now." Astrid considered Josian's pampered life with her lawyer husband. *Different lives* was a serious understatement. Still, though, Josian remained her closest companion. During the lean years after Astrid's apprenticeship, Josian surely would have taken her in if she'd known about her friend's bleak situation, but pride had prevented Astrid from asking. She had repaid her debt to Cecily and never borrowed again.

"Is she the reason you're part of Edwina's little business group?"

Astrid looked up. "You mean Tea and Talk?" God, even the name was juvenile, but she felt an inexplicable need to defend it. "It's not just a little business group, you know. We can't get into the London Business Council or the IFCT like men can. We have to make do."

Eli held up a hand. "I didn't mean any insult. I was curious what brought you there. You didn't exactly...fit in." He seemed to have chosen those last words carefully, perhaps worried about offending her.

"I'm not sure what you mean." Maybe was this about her appearance. She resisted the urge to look down at her dress.

Eli lingered on his wine glass for a moment before speaking. "I love my cousin. Edwina is earnest, kind, and perfectly respectable. But she's also mundane, and conservative, and even a bit...boring. Most of the women in that gaggle seemed to be of her ilk. I suppose most of us businesspeople are that way." He paused, an expression passing quickly over his face. "You're not like that."

Was that a compliment or not? Unsure whether or not to thank him, Astrid waited, hoping he would continue.

Setting down his glass, Eli rested his chin on his hand again, meeting Astrid's eyes. "When I first saw you, I knew you were different. Then you had the audacity to speak to me like you did, confirming my suspicions."

Remembering her angry outburst, Astrid looked down at her intertwined fingers, abashed. "I suppose I wasn't the picture of decorum, was I?"

Eli laughed, a short bark that made her look up in surprise. "No. But you intrigued me. No one speaks to me like that. And I don't speak like that to anyone." He said the last line with something like regret, and there it was again—a flash of emotion. Shame? Astrid peered more closely, but it was gone, his face projecting polite interest again. Dinner was illuminating some aspects of his personality and muddling others.

"And here we are. In this very, very classy restaurant." Astrid looked around at the gold chandeliers, the pressed white linens, the gentlemen and ladies conversing in hushed tones. "Did you hope that by bringing me here, you could make sure I'd behave?"

Eli's smile was shy, his dark eyes twinkling in the low

light. "Perhaps. I'm not very good with people making scenes."

"It's not going to work, you know. I'm a hard woman to control." Astrid returned his grin.

Eli nodded as the waiter arrived with their meals. "I'm starting to realize that."

13

―――――

Eli waited impatiently in the new workshop for Astrid to arrive. He couldn't remember the last time he was so excited, and he scolded himself for it. This was supposed to just be business, partnering with Astrid to solve a problem he couldn't solve on his own. He should not be so nervous about what she would think.

Although he was expecting it, the doorbell made him jump. He forced himself to walk casually up the stairs, rather than race, and waited a moment at the top before opening the door.

The night was drizzly but not rainy enough for an umbrella, and the green wool of Astrid's cloak was dappled with a fine mist. Over her left arm she carried a worn leather bag of tools. Stepping over the threshold, she pulled back her hood, shaking out her short brown hair.

"You found the place easily, then?" He'd managed to find a location only a half mile away from her home, wishing for her to feel comfortable there. She didn't seem to notice the hand he held out for her tool bag, so he dropped it back to his side, wanting her approval while trying not to want it.

"It wasn't hard. I've never been to this part of the neighborhood before, though." She looked around the entryway. "So where is it?"

"Come with me." Nearly giddy, he led her down the dark staircase and flung open the door at the bottom.

As she followed him inside, her expression went from anticipatory to confused. Though she'd probably been expecting a workshop, they were actually standing in a small flat. She looked around at her surroundings, eyes traveling from the worn sofa and chairs near the front door, to the fire burning in the fireplace grate, to the dining room table and small kitchen.

At last, she turned to him, eyebrows knitted in puzzlement. "I don't understand. This is a flat."

Taking her hand, he led her into what had once been a bedroom but was now a workshop. On one of the two long workbenches, he had already set out blueprint paper and pencils, straight edges, T-squares, and other design tools. Hand tools lined another wall along with steel shelving units filled with brass piping and buckets of miscellaneous cogs and gears. The room was well lit, gas lanterns spaced evenly along the walls and magnified by mirrors to throw light into every corner.

"What do you think?" He swept his arm around the space. When she hesitated, he kept talking. "It was a flat, yes, but the owners haven't been able to rent it on account of it being in the basement, so they agreed to let me redo the bedroom into a workshop." She should like it. This was the riskiest venture he'd undertaken, but for someone like her, a person who lived on the knife-edge of business risk all the time, maybe this was nothing special.

When she turned back to him, though, her smile lit up her face. "It's perfect." She set her bag of tools on one of the worktables and began exploring, poking through the buckets of parts, examining the hand tools. "How in the world did you get this put together so quickly? It's only been a few days."

"I called in some favors." He glossed over the truth, that he'd paid premiums and had workers in here setting up for two days straight, but he'd wanted her to be surprised. Her obvious excitement made the investment worth the expense.

"And this space is ours as long as we need it?"

Eli nodded. "I thought about only renting it through the end of May, which is the Judges' Viewing, but I didn't know if we might need it after that, so I rented it through the first week of June just to be sure. I figure we'd better be finished by then, what with the opening night of the Fair."

Astrid finished her inspection then drew up a stool at the table and pulled out her plans. "Well, then, we'd better win."

Eli took a seat right beside her and tacked down the corners of the large blueprint. She smelled good. Her proximity tempted him into dangerous thoughts, like what it would be like to kiss the curve of her neck. To distract himself, he began to fiddle with a pencil. "Let's talk about this design."

Astrid scanned the drawing. "What do you mean?"

"What's our ultimate goal for this machine?"

"That it wins the World's Fair, obviously." Astrid gave him a look that implied she thought he'd suddenly lost his wits.

"No, you misunderstand me." He tapped the sheet with his pencil. "I mean, what do we want this machine to do? What's our desired outcome?" He leaned his head on his hand, elbow resting on the table, and looked directly into her eyes, which narrowed as she considered his question.

Astrid licked her lips. "Pleasure. It's supposed to be the ultimate pleasure machine."

Eli would keep his thoughts on business, despite this topic of conversation. "And what gives a woman pleasure?"

Astrid paused. "Are you asking me what feels good?"

Yes, he wanted desperately to know that. If he was to lean across the space between them and capture her lips with his, would she kiss back? Would she moan into his mouth, slipping one hand up to twist in his hair? "You can answer hypothetically if you want. You're the expert. You build tools for this purpose all the time."

Astrid traced the curved outline of the drawing with her fingertip. "The clitoris is an essential component to the woman's sexual satisfaction." She cast him a sidelong glance with one raised eyebrow. "I assume you've heard of it?"

Oh, cheeky. "Yes, thanks. We've met."

Returning her gaze to the paper, she smiled. "Just making sure. Most men haven't."

Apparently she wanted to go down that road. "That's a pretty big assumption."

Astrid's smirk didn't fade. "Listen, if all gentlemen knew where the clitoris was, I wouldn't be selling so many felicitation machines to unhappy women."

She had a point.

Astrid picked up her own pencil and tapped the end against her lips, thinking, and his cock twitched inside his trousers. Those soft lips, sliding down the length of his shaft... Hell, he should not be thinking of this. She was talking, and he forced his attention back to her. "...so clitoral stimulation is key. A woman can certainly handle that herself, but if we're designing a machine to take care of business, it should *really* take care of business."

"Is it better to do it yourself, or for the machine to do it for you?" The question slipped out before he'd even thought about whether or not it was appropriate. He'd been wondering since first hearing about her felicitation devices. "Or maybe if *someone else* does it for you?"

Astrid tapped her pencil against her lips again. She was actually going to answer his too-personal question. "For me, it depends on my mood. I always know what I like. There's no guessing required. I don't have to hope someone else hits the right spot or try to explain exactly what I'm looking for. But the surprise is nice sometimes too. I don't get the surprise when I'm doing it myself."

He pressed on. "But what about the machines? That's a different situation, isn't it?"

"My products don't get tired. And they leave my hands free for other purposes. I have too many sensitive areas to not try to reach all of them." When she smiled at him, eyes sparkling and full of mischief, it was all he could do not to bend her over the worktable right there. Damn these urges. He hadn't felt lust—pure, unbridled lust—in a long time. Now, when he needed to focus, such urges were especially unwelcome. This was a dangerous path he was treading; he was starting to want her, and he certainly couldn't have her.

With effort, he brought himself back to the moment. She'd been talking about hands-free pleasure. He cleared his throat. "So the machine needs to provide—"

"—clitoral stimulation, yes. A ridge, or knob, or something similar. Very important."

"All right." Eli sketched a ridge onto her design where he imagined it would need to be, deliberately not thinking how it would nestle between her folds, pressing against her and making her gasp. He licked his dry lips and looked back up. "What else?"

Astrid tapped the place where she'd drawn the shaft on the saddle. "Penetration. It feels good to be fucked."

Eli blinked, his composure at risk of dissolving completely. "All right. I'll take your word on that. I've...wondered what it's like for you women."

Astrid bit her lower lip and smirked. "There are ways for you to find out."

Of course she would take it in that direction when he was trying to keep himself together. The "no" was on his lips, but he paused, imagining what it would be like to yield to her in that way. Eli hesitated only a moment, but it was enough for Astrid's smirk to go from teasing to completely devilish.

He shook his head, skin burning up. It was far too hot in here. "It's not the same, and you know it."

Astrid shrugged. "Suit yourself. But you have all sorts of parts that I don't have and can't relate to, so I guess we're even. Besides, that's why we can have so much fun together." She paused then added, "I mean hypothetical couples can have so much fun together, of course."

"Of course." She might be trying to seduce him, or she might be just flirting. He wasn't used to women being so forward. Wasn't used to flirting at all, actually. Not anymore.

Astrid looked back down at the design. "I suppose that's everything, right?"

Eli looked at her, incredulous. "That's it? You have some amazing machines back at your flat, and you want the bare minimum for this? That's not exciting at all. I thought you were more creative than this. I guess I was wrong." He shook his head in mock disapproval.

Astrid tossed her pencil down onto the table and folded her arms. "All right. As the person who is not the target audience for this machine, tell me what we're missing."

"No, you're the expert here, apparently. You tell me."

Their eyes met and locked, neither looking away, each challenging the other to take this further. Astrid smiled, then, a catlike, predatory smile that sent a sudden thrill of anxiety through him. She leaned closer. "Maybe I should tell you what turns me on. For the sake of our research."

She was so close, a rosy blush spreading across her face, across her collarbones, down to swells of her breasts, and his hands ached to touch her. But...no. This was a terrible idea. "I don't think that's appropriate, Astrid."

Instead of pulling away, she moved even closer, resting her hand casually on his thigh, the warmth burning right through his trousers. "Come on, Eli. Nothing we're doing is appropriate."

"That's the problem." Brushing her hand away, he scooted back, flustered and unsettled. "What are you getting at, here?"

Astrid rested her chin on her hand, leaning on the worktable. "You can deny it all you want, but there's something here between us. And that pisses me off more than anything else, since you're prudish and self-righteous and more than a bit sexist, and I'd like nothing more than to keep you at a distance. But since that clearly isn't going to happen, I figure we might as well fuck and get it out of our systems."

He stared at her, his mouth going dry. Fantasies he'd been trying to put aside flooded through his mind: taking her hard against the wall, her head thrown back in ecstasy, her tight pussy clenching around his cock, and her breathy little moans in his ears. Swallowing hard, he fought to gather his composure, to find something to say, but just ended up opening and closing his mouth without saying anything.

For a moment, her flirtatious veneer fell away and vulnerability flashed across her face. Then she looked away, pulling her hand back, the walls going up so swiftly, he could practically see her shut those feelings away. "If you don't want to, then fine. I thought you were attracted to me."

He laughed, a short, incredulous bark of disbelief, getting to his feet. "You think I'm not attracted to you?" And before he could stop himself, before he could remember all the reasons why this was a terrible idea, he pulled her up to her feet and crushed her mouth to his.

God, she tasted so sweet, her lips as soft and yielding as he had imagined. Her hands trembled on his shoulders, only a moment's hesitation before she wrapped her arms around him. He kissed her soundly, cupping her head with one hand to keep her close, holding her firmly against him with one arm wrapped around her waist. Her lips parted, and he ran his tongue against hers, angling his head to deepen the kiss. The blood pounded in his body, his desire a tangible force. He slid one hand down over the curve of her bottom, and she moaned into his mouth.

Eli wanted more, now, wanted to take Astrid on the workbench or on the floor, to unfasten her corset and hike up her skirt and have her gasping and clenching around him. His cock ached just from this kiss, and she arched into him, pressing her softness into the hard line of his erection.

Awareness crashed over him like a cold wave. He shouldn't

start down this path. Drawing back, breathless, he practically pushed her away from him as he struggled to compose himself. She stared up at him, dazed, blinking heavy-lidded eyes.

"I can't do this." He turned away, steadying himself. "I can't take advantage of you."

Whatever response he was expecting, it wasn't laughter. She started giggling behind her hand, mirth twinkling in her eyes.

"Is something funny?" The question came out more sharply than he intended, but she still seemed amused.

"It's just that you're such a prude!"

"Will you stop saying that?" Anger blossomed in his chest as he tried not to think of other times he'd been called the same.

"I'm sorry. You really think you're taking advantage of me?" Astrid looked skyward, still laughing. "I've been trying to seduce you since I walked in here."

"But your reputation. You can't take a strange man home with you."

"Of course I can. What year do you think this is?" Astrid hopped up on the worktable, legs dangling freely. "Eli, you can hang on to whatever outdated notions of propriety work for you in your world, but I'm not going to deny myself what I want just because I'm worried about what people will think."

Taking deep, calming breaths, he studied her. Maybe she had a point. Maybe it wasn't his responsibility to protect her reputation. He wanted to believe her.

Astrid licked her lips. "I'm only talking about one night. Resolve this tension between us, and then we can get back to work like normal."

It was tempting. He hesitated, running through the pros and cons in his mind. She was so damn sexy, sitting there swinging her feet, her dark eyes sparkling in the light from the lanterns. He'd sworn off relationships after Mallory, wasn't going to go through that heartache again. But Astrid was proposing sex. She wasn't proposing a relationship—and he wasn't surprised; she was dynamic, bold, adventurous, and he was a straightforward businessman like every other business-man. If sex didn't mean anything, they could share one night and be done with it. No heartache, no complications.

"Just one night. One night, and this never happens again." He ran a hand through his hair. "Right?"

"Of course. You're still a self-righteous prude, and I doubt I'd be able to stand more than one night." Her smile indicated that she was teasing, but she'd made it clear what she thought of him already.

He looked around the workshop. "So…what happens now, exactly?"

Astrid hopped down off her perch. "Now, you take me home."

14

———

Astrid had a half-mile walk and four flights of stairs to reconsider, but she definitely wanted to take Eli Rutledge to bed, right then. They walked mostly in silence, neither willing to break the spell. When they finally reached her flat, she fumbled with the lock on her door before sliding it home and stepping inside.

When she turned to him, she knew at once he was having second thoughts. He leaned against the closed door, hands in his trouser pockets, looking around as if he hadn't seen the flat a few days earlier. Hands on her hips, she waited for him to process whatever protest he was considering. At last he asked, "Astrid, are you sure about this?"

"Yes. Are you?"

"One night." He held up a finger for emphasis.

She nodded, managing not to roll her eyes. "One night."

"Then back to business." He ran a hand through his hair, as he always seemed to do when he was nervous.

"All work and no play, just the way you like it."

He ignored her comment, seeming to steel himself, his

shoulders tensing and then relaxing, as if preparing for some great test. "All right."

Then, all trace of his restraint vanished. He stepped into her, pressing her back against the closed door, his body flush against hers as he kissed her again. Arousal sizzled through her as his mouth moved seamlessly from her lips to her jaw and up to her ear, nipping at the tender skin of her earlobe. He whispered, "God, I want to fuck you so badly." That word in the husky voice of the prim and proper Eli Rutledge made her legs wobbly. She'd expected to be leading the way, but he kissed as if he was well versed in it, and she yielded immediately. His breath brushed hot against her neck as he slid his lips down to her throat. She'd forgotten the thrill of a rough beard against her skin, and she shivered in his arms.

As Eli dipped his tongue into the hollow of her throat, Astrid leaned her head back against the door, hands reflexively clutching his shoulder blades. He nipped her collarbone, first gently, then harder, making her whimper. Yes, wherever he had learned to do this, he was definitely no novice. Eli's hand slid from her back to the curve of her arse, then he hitched one of her legs up over his hip and lifted her up on tiptoe. His erection rubbed her clit through the thin fabric of her skirt, the friction enough to wring another gasp from her. Yes, more of *that*. She pressed against him, each movement sparking a frisson of pleasure.

When he stepped back, she moaned at the loss of contact, but he was only tugging her farther into the room, his lips returning to hers. "Where is your bed?" he asked against her mouth.

It only took a minute to drag him into the bedroom and push him down onto the bed. She climbed on him, straddling his hips, her skirt riding up her thighs. He ran his hands up beneath her skirt and stopped when he found skin, his face lighting up with a smile. "This is what you wore to our workshop? No underthings?"

"I'm a fan of convenience."

His fingers played with the upper edge of her stockings, tracing her garters, and she shifted slightly to press down against his hardness again, looking for that delicious friction. The pressure wrung a groan from him, his fingers tightening almost painfully against her legs. So he liked that, did he? She leaned down to kiss him and rocked her hips forward, feeling his cock twitch in his pants.

Eli drew back from the kisses to look at her, really look at her, in a way that made Astrid flush all over. He scooted back until he was sitting up against her headboard, gaze skimming her body as she moved forward with him. She couldn't remember the last time someone had looked at her that way, with pure, untamed lust. His gaze made her skin hot, her mind dizzy.

"Let's slow things down," he murmured, voice husky, and traced a finger down the front hooks of her corset. "I want to watch you take this off."

Eli's eyes followed the movement of her fingers as she unfastened each hook and eye, finally letting the whole corset fall behind her. Her blouse was loose and nearly sheer, and his hungry gaze roamed over her breasts visible beneath it. Before he could reach up to touch her, she began unbuttoning the coat he still wore and pushed it down off his shoulders. Then she moved on to his vest and starched high-collared shirt.

Eli's breathing quickened beneath her fingers as she brushed his chest, undoing each button, his white undershirt soon the only garment between his skin and her touch. It had been a long time since she'd touched a man like this, and after she slid his shirt off his shoulders, she ran both hands up his arms. The tight muscles moved beneath her hands, his forearms sinewy with lean strength.

Before she could continue, Eli lifted her off him and slid out from under her. He took a moment to remove his shoes and set them aside. Then he knelt in front of her and began unfastening her boots. His eyes didn't leave hers as he slid her boots off, his fingers tracing the stockings that covered her calves. She'd never considered boot removal sexy before, but when he placed a kiss on the inside of her knee, she had to press her lips together to stifle a cry.

Still kneeling, Eli took hold of the hem of her blouse and pulled it up and over her head. Astrid lifted her hips to allow him to slide her skirt off, the action leaving her naked except for her stockings and garter belt. Eli exhaled in a long, slow, measured way as he stared, taking her in, his gaze raking over her. A man's stare should not have the power to make her come undone, but her body throbbed as if he were touching her. She lay back on the bed and enjoyed the delicious thrill of having him watch her. She put one arm behind her head and draped the other across her stomach.

"You look…God, you look fucking incredible." The timbre of his voice made her throb. He lay down next to her, still mostly clothed, and brought his mouth to hers again.

Eyes closed, Astrid yielded to the incredible feelings as Eli stroked his palm across her breasts, touching each in turn, cupping them reverently. At first, he touched gently, cautiously, the brush of his thumb across her nipple barely enough to feel. Before she could ask for more, though, he pinched harder, and at her moan, harder again, gauging her reaction and swallowing her sighs and whimpers. Then he bent his head to her breast.

Fuck, he was *really* good at this. Astrid clutched his scalp as he bit and sucked at her nipples, sending sharp bursts of pleasure through her. His lips and teeth moved with practiced ease, teasing the sensitive flesh until she began to squirm beneath him. Her body burned with the desire for more.

His lips curled up against her skin. "Take it easy." Opening her eyes, she watched Eli pull off his undershirt, revealing a muscular chest dusted with dark-brown curls. As she reached up to touch him, Eli caught her hand in his. "Not yet. I'm not through with you." Before she could reach out to him again, he moved to sit between her legs, parting them gently but firmly. His insistent gaze down at her folds sent another flood of arousal through her, the indecency of their situation setting her aflame. This man seemed completely different from the Eli who shied away from her in their workshop. How had she ever thought him a prude?

Astrid couldn't help but gasp when he pressed his fingertip against her clit, the sudden sensation making her toes curl. A tiny part of her brain confirmed that he seemed no stranger at all to the clitoris, nor to any of her other parts, either.

He began to rub her clit in small circles. "Does that feel good?"

She couldn't speak coherently if he was going to keep doing that. "Mmm," she managed, a murmur that turned into a moan as he pressed one finger slowly into her, then a second.

"You're so wet, Astrid." He slowly stroked his fingers in and out, curling them up on each stroke, and she could do nothing but ball her fists in the blankets and try not to pant. Someone had taught him how to do this, and she wanted to thank whoever it had been.

When he withdrew both fingers to slide them into his mouth, she nearly lost her mind. None of the men she'd been with ever wanted to taste her, but the intimacy of the act made her quiver. She wanted to touch him, now, to return the pleasure, but when she went to sit up, he pushed her back down.

"Not yet. I said I'm not finished here." With a few quick flicks of the wrist, he unfastened her garter belt, and the ease with which he did so belied any of his earlier conservative behavior. Eli Rutledge had definitely done that more than a few times before. She put the thought aside as he rolled the stockings down, revealing her knees, calves, and feet. He then ran his hands slowly up her legs, tracing her skin with his fingertips, lingering on her inner thighs. She quivered with anticipation when he drew his finger up through her folds again and knew from his smile that he could feel her trembling. Then, after bending down, he kissed her stomach right above her curls and then a bit lower. There, he paused, his lips only inches from where she desperately wanted them.

"Has anyone ever done this for you before?" he asked, breath hot against her folds.

Someone with his head between her legs definitely deserved the truth. "No man has."

When he caught her meaning, he drew back, his eyes widening as he smiled. "I see. I imagine your standards are fairly high, then." With just a fingertip, he brushed against her again, and she arched reflexively as her head fell back.

"Just...just...please..." She waved her hand in a "go on"

motion, and he smiled before lowering his mouth to her.

The first touch of his lips was light, delicate, barely perceptible to her senses. On the next touch, he swiped his tongue straight up across her clit, and she arched against him with a cry as dizzying pleasure rushed over her. Oh, *yes*. He focused on her tight bud, laving it slowly and firmly with his tongue, and she couldn't stop pressing up to his mouth with each stroke. It was so good, intimate and overwhelmingly hot, and her entire body tingled as he switched from licking to sucking on her clit. His beard scraped against her folds, and the touch of his coarse hairs against her tender skin made all thought leave her, because that was new and *wonderful*.

As he slid two fingers into her again, she began babbling and couldn't stop. "Oh God…oh God…Eli…oh fuck…fuck…*fuck*…" When he pressed upward, finding that fantastic spot that made her vision white out, she could no longer find words, could barely breathe as he expertly pushed her closer and closer to climax. His lips moved over her in no rush, pleasuring her with methodical and deliberate precision, clearly enjoying driving her out of her mind. She grabbed the covers again as her whole world dissolved to the sensations between her legs. She was close, beginning the steady, inexorable climb to the point of no return, her peak shimmering out of reach but washing ever closer with each stroke of his tongue or press of his fingers.

When he sucked hard on her clit, her whole world exploded. She arched up into his mouth, wracked with spasms, the climax more intense than she had felt in a long time, maybe in forever, and he was right there, taking her through it, holding her in the throes of ecstasy for longer than she thought possible.

At last she came back to herself, barely able to catch her breath, and opened her eyes. Eli lay stretched out next to her, his hand resting on her hip. He hadn't even undressed yet, still wearing his trousers. Astrid couldn't think of a witty comeback or any kind of comment at all. The only thing she could do was exhale, slowly and shakily, and continue to lose herself in those dark eyes.

"How was that?" He sounded hesitant, his eyebrows raised in genuine interest as though he didn't realize he'd just driven her out of her mind with his fingers and tongue. He had to be kidding…unless he didn't know his own talents.

Astrid had regained enough sense of self to flirt, to play, to make some impish or sarcastic comment, but games seemed ridiculous, so she just smiled and didn't answer. Without further preamble, she reached for his trouser buttons, helping him out of the rest of his clothes. He let her, lifting his hips so she could undress him. When at last he was naked, she straddled his thighs to examine his cock.

As someone who made imitations for a living, she was qualified to judge it fantastic: precisely the right length, maybe a tad thicker than she was expecting, well-shaped, and hard as steel. He let her study him, but his amused smile changed to a slack-jawed groan when she took him in hand.

She rubbed her thumb over the tip and was rewarded by his head lolling back with pleasure, eyelids fluttering. With her other hand, she cupped his sac as she began stroking his shaft from root to tip, loving the way his hips moved to press into her hand. After only a few minutes, his hip thrusts grew more erratic, and he reached down to stop her. He was beginning to come undone, and the feral expression on his face was enough to make her spasm inside. She leaned down to kiss him, his erection pressing between them.

Eli took her breasts in his hands again and flicked his thumbs across the nipples. "I want to be inside you," he said against her lips.

Astrid drew back. "Give me a minute." She climbed off him, deliberately brushing against his erection as she passed, and turned to her bedside table drawer.

Behind her, he ran his fingers down her spine, tracing the spiral of stars tattooed there. "These are beautiful."

"I thought it was appropriate. My name, and all that." She opened the drawer, and he sat up to watch what she was doing.

Leaning over her, he peered at the clutter of products. "A bit of a collector, are you?"

Astrid smiled. "I keep the originals." A small, decorative brass box in the back of the drawer held her pessary. As she lay back to slip the pessary inside herself, Eli began to poke around in the drawer. She let him. Even though he was clearly no stranger to a woman's body, he was new to felicitation devices.

When he continued to look through her inventions, Astrid cleared her throat. "Are you almost finished?"

With a sheepish smile, he closed the drawer and rolled back over to her, making amends by kissing her again. She could kiss this man all day, and for the first time, she felt a pang of regret that this was a one-night event. Deliberately putting that dangerous thought out of her mind, she slid one hand down his back, guiding him on top of her. Without breaking their kiss, he settled himself between her open legs, rocking forward to rub against her.

Astrid whimpered into his mouth. The hard grind of his shaft against her clit made her clench. She lifted her hips to him, seeking that feeling again. Eli propped himself up on his elbows, holding his body above her, hesitating with his cock poised right at her entrance. Staring down into her eyes, he slid all the way inside.

They both gasped at the same time. He was just the right size, wide enough that she felt stretched taut and the perfect length to bury himself completely to the hilt in her warmth. Her muscles were already quivering around him, milking his cock, and he held himself fully enveloped for a moment, motionless, his breath coming short and fast as he rested his head against her neck. When he spoke, his rough voice broke. "I love the way you feel."

His words made her tighten around him. After her recent orgasm, she was so much more sensitive, and when he pulled out of her, every inch of his hard cock lit her nerves on fire. She met him thrust for thrust, rocking her hips up, the angle pressing his body against her clit with each stroke. He didn't rush, fucking her as though they had all night, each push deep and hard and perfect.

Eli lowered his mouth to her breast and began to suck on her nipple, dragging it between his teeth as he rolled the other nipple between his fingers. The sparks of pleasure were already building, already carrying her back to the edge. Her pussy clenched around him, orgasm imminent, the heavy, throbbing anticipation turning her bones to liquid.

He was hitting all the right spots, and she couldn't help crying out as he bit harder on her nipple.

When she came, her entire frame convulsed so strongly that she arched up off the bed, both hands digging into his shoulders. Eli released her nipple with a moan as her muscles clenched around him. He thrust hard, his hands tight on her hips, and exploded inside her with a groan. Through the haze, she could feel his body trembling as he emptied himself, flooding her with warmth. At last, he collapsed on her, breathing heavily into her neck, his cock still buried inside her.

In the haze of afterglow, Astrid stroked Eli's hair, relishing his weight on top of her. He seemed in no hurry to move. She ran one hand down his back, moving across the strong muscles beneath the skin, and he shivered, dropping a light kiss on her neck. "That feels nice." With that, he rolled off her. Astrid sat up, sluggish with satisfaction. This part was always a little uncertain. To delay the awkwardness, she got out of bed to clean up.

When she returned, Eli had pulled his trousers back on and was lounging back on the bed, arms folded behind his head, looking sated. She sat down next to him. "That was fun," she said.

He smiled. "You know, it was. Maybe this was just the thing for us. Getting the tension out of our system and all that."

"Of course." Astrid looked past him at the wall, knowing exactly how counterproductive this night had been for her in that measure. Eli Rutledge was more firmly entrenched in her "system" than ever before. She wanted to lay him back down and fuck him again, wanted to hold him in her arms for the whole night. Instead, she turned to the question at the front of her mind. "So who was she?"

Eli turned his head to look at her, eyebrows raised. "Who was who?"

Astrid settled down on her side next to him, propping herself up on her elbow. "The woman who taught you all that. You've never been to the Lahey Emporium, so you probably didn't learn from a brothel, and nobody knows how to do those things without instruction."

Eli looked away, confirming Astrid's suspicions. "I did see professional women, back when I was younger. Before I had a reputation to protect."

Astrid was good at reading people, her line of work lending itself to observation. "That isn't everything, though." When he continued to hesitate, she touched his arm. "You can tell me. It's all right."

Eli stared up at the ceiling. "I was engaged once. To a woman named Mallory."

The tangle of emotions inside Astrid was hard to tease apart. Curiosity, interest, and a bit of jealousy, yes, but maybe something else, somewhere down inside. "What happened?"

"She ended it. I guess she never really wanted to marry me. Her family had been pushing her into the whole thing. They wanted the business connections and status that would come from marrying into Rutledge Handiworks." He shrugged, the gesture awkward since he was lying on his back. "I thought she loved me. She loved parts of me, anyway." He snorted in a self-deprecating way. "She never wanted to set a date for the wedding. Kept putting it off, putting it off, and finally, when I pushed the issue, she admitted she had no intention of marrying me."

"She led you on?" Astrid had words for people like that, people who lied about their romantic or sexual intentions. "Did she fall in love with someone else?"

Eli continued to stare at the ceiling, arms folded behind his head, not answering. Finally, he exhaled a long breath through his nose. "She said that no matter how well she taught me to fuck, I'd always be a stuck-up businessman like her father. And that's how it ended." He swallowed. "It was a long time ago."

His eyes were tight. "But it still bothers you," Astrid said.

Eli tipped his head to the side. "She was right, though. Mallory wanted a life full of adventure and excitement, and I provide none of those things. Women like that..." His voice trailed off as he searched for the right words, looking up to her ceiling again as he finished. "They don't want to be saddled down with watch salesmen." His smile was self-deprecating, and he looked back into her eyes. "It's best for me that she left. At least I hadn't married her."

Astrid leaned over and kissed him again. She wasn't sure why she was doing it, whether she needed to comfort him or herself. He kissed her back, tenderly, without heat. Pulling back, she absentmindedly ran a tongue over her bottom lip, and he watched her. Realizing what she was doing, she turned away and sat up.

Eli seemed to read her hesitation. "Do you want me to leave now?"

Astrid looked down at her own nakedness, self-conscious all of a sudden. "That was our deal, wasn't it?"

"Our deal was one night." When he paused, Astrid looked over at him, and he was watching her. "I guess that's open to interpretation."

Her heart fluttered with renewed hope, but that didn't have to mean anything. She just enjoyed having sex with him. "I wouldn't mind if you stayed."

Did he look so eager because he wanted sex again? Or was there something else in those eyes? "It *is* pretty late."

"That's true." Astrid lay back beside him. His body was so firm and warm. Unable to resist, she slipped a hand down to his cock, which was already half hard again.

Eli jumped. "What are you doing?"

She faltered. "I thought if you were interested, I might want to get you out of my system again."

When she met his eyes, he was smiling. Without answering, he pulled her on top of him and tugged her down for another kiss.

JOSIAN'S first letter arrived the following morning shortly after Eli left. Astrid had been standing in the living room, staring at the closed door with a mixture of emotions, when a loud *thwump* behind her jolted her out of her reverie. After pulling the canister from its delivery tube, she noted the return address scrawled across the glass with a grease pencil. She unscrewed the canister and pulled out a piece of crisp, lavender stationery.

MY DEAREST ASTRID—

I do hope you're doing well. We're all settled here in Mortonshire, at last. I always forget how gloomy it is until we're unpacked and the house is opened up, but now the sun is shining and I finally have a moment to write to you.

How are your plans for the World's Fair? Do you have an idea yet? The deadline is coming up so soon. I'm trying to convince Warren to return in time for opening night, but he has a cricket tournament sched-uled for that same day and I doubt we will make it. Please don't be cross with me.

And speaking of being cross, please consider apologizing to Eli Rutledge. He has many connections in the business world, and it would not be advantageous to make him your adversary. I know you're proud, but the consequences could be far-reaching.

It's time for tea now, so I must go. Please write soon.

Yours, Josian

ASTRID SMILED at the paper before sitting down at the desk with her own plain stationery. She had to sweep aside some gears to make a place to write.

DEAR JOSIAN,

It's so nice to hear from you, as always. I hope you enjoy your time up at Mortonshire. Don't let Warren drag you to too many dull events, all right? It's your vacation as well.

I'm quite busy now with preparations for the World's Fair. I do have an idea, but I don't want to write much about it now. Let me just say that it's a much grander undertaking than I've ever anticipated.

HER PEN HOVERED over the paper, and then she added another line to her letter.

DON'T WORRY about Eli Rutledge. I've apologized.

15

———

He and Astrid had arranged to meet just after noon on Sunday, but Eli arrived at their workshop an hour early with two large bags of supplies. He felt rested, finally, having caught up on the sleep he'd lost Friday night. Working in his shop on Saturday had been brutal, battling exhaustion while trying to look cheerful for customers after having gotten no sleep at all the previous night. He'd made himself go shopping, though, wanting to surprise Astrid with the machinery they'd need to build their device.

Astrid. Eli paused in unpacking the supplies to recall his night with her, reveling in the memory of her body beneath his, her face as she came. He had relived that night a dozen times in the intervening day, enough to know he was in over his head. He was sure one night had not been enough to dispel the tension between them. Previously, he had been able to put her from his mind, but now he couldn't stop thinking of her. Her scent was in his clothes and on his skin, his cock rising to attention at completely inopportune times during the workday. Despite his exhaustion, he'd had to bring himself off when he got home in order to sleep.

He returned to unpacking supplies, smiling despite himself. Sleeping with Astrid may have been a bad decision, but he couldn't make himself regret it. At least he would have the memories, since he couldn't allow himself anything else. Girls like Astrid were adventurous, spirited, courageous, and eventually they would grow tired of men like him.

"Hi."

Her voice behind him made him jump, bumping the work-table where he'd laid out all their equipment. Turning, he saw her standing in the doorway, looking hesitant. Maybe she'd spent previous day questioning their night together. Or worse, regretting it. Maybe she wondered if *he* regretted it. He smiled, wanting to allay any fears she might have. "I didn't even hear you come in."

"I suppose the front door is pretty quiet." She set her bags of tools down on the workbench. "What's all this?"

"I picked up a few things. Wanted to get here early and set up."

"I guess we both had the same idea. Seems like you beat me." Astrid began to poke through the gears Eli had set out on the table. "How did you know what to get?"

"I had to guess. I figure it's enough to get started." Rubbing his beard, he studied the purchases. Maybe he had too presumptuous. "I wanted to be helpful."

"I appreciate it." She smiled up at him. "I guess we should start."

At first, Eli lost himself in the work. They decided to focus on the saddle, which involved so much labor that he could distract himself from her scent. Between the shaping, fastening, and sanding, they worked well into the afternoon without making much discernible headway. They also worked in near silence, and he couldn't determine if she was focused or maybe uncomfortable after their night together. But there was no use in wondering; the night was behind them, and they had a task to do.

When they took a break for lunch, Eli considered their progress. The saddle shape was coming together, albeit more slowly than he'd expected. Astrid was apparently thinking the same thing. "When do you think we'll get it finished?"

Eli leaned back on the worn sofa. "Later this week, maybe. We have enough time if we work diligently, I think. The Judges' Viewing is still almost three weeks away."

Astrid tapped her fingertips against her lips, bringing to mind the feeling of those lips against his and an overwhelming urge to have that again. He took a sip of water to hide the wave of emotions. Astrid seemed oblivious, staring off toward their workroom down the hall. "This is just the mock-up," Astrid said. "Our final one is going to be made out of metal, not wood, so that might take even longer. All that soldering and welding. We should leave enough time for that."

"But we'll have the mock-up to work from, so that will make things easier." Eli imagined how it would look, picturing the finished design from their drawings. Then, he imagined Astrid riding it the way she had ridden him, her head thrown back, crying out in pleasure.

Astrid finished her sandwich and tea. "Ready to get back to it?"

Eli nodded, his pants uncomfortably tight. "Ready."

By the time evening arrived, they had at least finished crafting the rough frame of the saddle. It was easy to lose track of time down there in the apartment without windows. When he checked his watch at last, growing weary, it was past six. He gestured to Astrid, who was working over the surface with a steam-powered sander, and asked if she was ready to wrap up for the evening.

"Almost. Let me finish this sanding."

Eli ran a hand over the smooth surface. "We're covering it with leather, right? It doesn't need to be so smooth."

Astrid brushed the hair out of her face and slid the goggles up her forehead. "I want it to be smooth before we start covering it, since we're going to need to test it for size."

Eli cleared a spot on the worktable around the saddle and offered her his hand. "Climb up. Let's take a look."

Astrid hesitated a moment before accepting his helping hand onto the workbench. After brushing the sawdust aside, she swung one leg over their base. Her skirt rode up on her thighs as she did so. Eli wondered if she was wearing any underthings.

Shifting slightly, Astrid frowned. "It's low."

"You can sit down on it. You have to lower yourself down."

She shook her head. "No, it should just fit when I kneel, I think. It would be even better if I couldn't quite reach, so my legs dangled a little. That way, all my weight would be on the device. Much better stimulation."

That mental image was going to be the death of him. He swallowed and nodded, hoping she wouldn't notice.

Astrid carefully climbed down from the saddle. "We need to raise it up."

"I suppose. You're the expert, after all."

"It's going to be heavy." She surveyed the device. "Maybe we should attach it to some kind of frame, so she doesn't have to maneuver it onto a table or bed." Astrid returned to their blueprints. "We don't want her to do the heavy lifting. It should be self-supporting."

"All right." Eli began to sketch legs on the drawing. "So she sits astride it?"

"Pads here and here." Astrid took a pencil and drew them in. "That way she can let her legs hang or kneel on the pads, but either way, full penetration. We can make the pads adjustable." She stifled a yawn. "I think you're right. We should wrap up for the evening."

The night was cool but clear, and as they walked back to Astrid's flat, Eli admired the few stars visible above the glow of the city. She walked so close to him that her hips brushed against his, and he wanted to wrap his arm around her waist but knew it was improper. These feelings were only because they'd been working so closely together that day. He hadn't been with a woman in too long, so Astrid was affecting him more than she normally would have.

At her door, Astrid extended her hand. "Wednesday, then? Around ten a.m.?"

Eli kissed her hand, wishing again that he were going inside her flat. "Ten a.m."

16

———

"Finally."

Eli's sigh of relief made Astrid turn. He pushed his goggles up onto the top of his head and set the welding gun aside, studying his creation with an expression of triumph. For the last two days, while Astrid had been constructing the vibrator, Eli had been working on the lever system and machinery for the thrusting shaft.

Astrid set down the vibrator motor she'd been finishing and walked over, pushing her own magnifying goggles up into her hair. "Is it done?" The contraption was a mess of levers and pulleys, but as she studied the layout, it began to make sense. "Looks like you've modulated speed, depth, and vibration?"

"I think so. I haven't turned it on yet." Eli rubbed his beard and chuckled sheepishly. "Sort of afraid it won't work."

"Only one way to find out." Astrid flipped the switch to fire up the motor. After a shuddering hesitation, it rumbled into life. The piston began to move up and down, up and down, driving an invisible cock they hadn't yet attached.

"Well, would you look at that." Eli shook his head in awe. "I can't believe it works." He adjusted a knob on one lever, and the movement slowed to a steady, methodical rhythm. A crank changed the height of the stroke. Watching the machine made Astrid desperate to test it out.

Ever since her night with Eli, she'd barely been able to keep her hands to herself. Rather than getting him out of her system, she'd thought of almost nothing else in the days since. She'd thrown herself into the work with fanatical passion, but every time Eli spoke to her or brushed up against her, she was distracted all over again. He'd seemed relieved when she'd suggested they work on separate projects; maybe he was as bothered as she was. She hoped he was—they should suffer equally.

One of the greatest benefits of working on separate projects was the time she was able to spend ogling his arse while he bent over the machine. Before their night together, she never appreciated this man's incredible body. It seemed a waste not to study its various planes and angles whenever she had a chance. As a result, it had taken her two full days to assemble the vibrating components of the machine when it really should only have taken a few hours. Fortunately, Eli hadn't seemed to notice her glacial work pace. He'd been so wrapped up in his own tasks that he'd completely ignored her other than at meal times.

She still couldn't tell how he was feeling about having slept with her, whether he regretted it or was eager for more. He had been hard to read since then, staying so focused on their build that he discussed nothing else. Maybe she was the one being obsessive while he was being professional. Every so often, though, she could feel him watching her, and when she looked, he returned immediately to his task. Maybe he was as distracted as she was. Or she was being ridiculous.

"Are you all right?"

Astrid snapped out of her reverie at the sound of his voice. "Hmm? What? I'm fine. Why?"

"I've been talking to you for the last minute and you've been staring at the machine." Eli switched it off and patted the seat. "Thinking about hopping up to give it a go?"

"Don't be ridiculous." She forced herself to laugh. "I'm nearly finished with the main vibrators. Why don't you get the attachments ready?"

Evening was upon them by the time they finished hooking up all the gearing and had the machine fully operational. Working so closely with Eli, Astrid was often pressed against him as they fastened complicated machinery; this contact distracted her more than she wanted to admit. When the last piece was soldered into place and the gears were turning properly, she stepped several paces away from him to catch her breath.

More distracting, however, was the sight of the machine fully operational. Even though this was just their prototype, they'd covered the saddle with leather, hiding the components and its unfinished wooden surface. The polished shaft rose up and down in an obscene pantomime. The thrusting, vibrating machine was both grotesque and oddly fascinating. Astrid couldn't look away. Beside her, Eli seemed likewise entranced.

"It's..." She searched for a word, could think of nothing. "Wow."

"I know." Eli pressed his palm against the vibrating ridge in front of the shaft. "Everything seems to be working." He rubbed the back of his hand across his forehead to clear some engine grease. "That's more than enough for one day. I think we should wrap up for tonight."

Astrid's work station was still a mess. "I'm building a different-size shaft to swap out with this one. It's nearly done. I think I'm going to stay around for a little while to finish it." When he glanced at his watch, she added, "I'll leave before it gets dark, don't worry. I'll be perfectly fine."

"Are you sure?"

"Of course." She flashed him what she hoped was a dazzling smile. "Just another half hour or so. I hate leaving work unfinished."

Eli frowned. "All right. When should we meet again?"

They made plans to meet that Sunday, which was ideal: Astrid needed a few days away from Eli to clear her head. He dawdled around after they finalized the plans, straightening up his work station, seeming reluctant to leave. Finally, Astrid had no choice but to ignore him and continue working on the alternate shaft that, at the moment, she didn't care at all about finishing. At last, Eli said his goodbyes and left.

With a rapidly beating heart, Astrid waited for at least ten minutes for him to come back to the flat with some excuse about having forgotten something. When he didn't reappear, she put her work aside in relief to deal with the real reason she'd stayed behind—she was going to test this machine.

Astrid took a moment to familiarize herself with the switches. A hand-crank adjusted the maximum height of the shaft at full penetration. Would she be able to reach the crank when she was seated? A quick examination told her no. That was a design flaw that would need fixing, and she made a note on her to-do list. Then she adjusted the crank to what she considered a reasonable height. After brushing the sawdust away from the machine, clearing a path for herself, she carefully climbed up onto the workbench.

Mounting the device was more complicated than she'd anticipated. With a bit of struggle, she rose awkwardly over the saddle, aligned herself appropriately, and carefully sank down onto the shaft.

Oh God. When fully impaled on the replica cock beneath her, Astrid's clit pressed down on the machine's ridge, her body weight holding her in place as her knees just brushed the worktable. She'd wanted the saddle to be taller, and now it was, and she couldn't move away without awkwardly climbing back up to a squatting position. She took a moment to catch her breath, fighting against the sudden, overwhelming sensation of being filled after days of unsatisfied arousal. If she wasn't careful, she could come just like this, shifting her hips to grind down against the leather. Satisfying, but inadequate as a test of the machine. She had to turn it on. With a deep breath, she reached down under the machine and turned the first dial.

The vibrations started first, rumbling directly against her cleft, wringing a gasp from her lips. With her legs spread like this, her exposed clit pressed hard against the unyielding leather. She needed something to hold on to and gripped the edge of the saddle in front of her, overwhelmed by the intense stimulation, trying not to come too quickly. With fading composure, she reached down to the other switch.

The shaft inside her seemed to shudder for a moment as the machinery kicked in, and then it steadily withdrew from her wet folds. When only the tip remained inside her, it reversed direction and began sliding all the way upward, driving deep into her. She'd just caught her breath when the cycle began all over again, up then down, while the ridge continued to vibrate against her clit. The slow, inexorable thrusts were more frustrating than fulfilling, and she needed more.

Reaching down beneath the lip of the saddle again, she found the dial that would increase the speed of the shaft. With a half turn, the penetrations sped up, the device fucking her faster. That was…incredible, nearly too much, completely merciless in its tireless motion. Astrid couldn't lift off the saddle, her position offering no leverage. *Fuck.* As the hard cock continued stroking into her over and over again, her climax built with breathtaking speed, bearing down on her like an unstoppable force. She usually liked to back off on the vibrations when she approached her peak, easing into the moment, but with this machine, that wasn't an option.

Her orgasm was torn out of her. Breathlessly, she crashed over the peak, clenching around the fake cock driving in and out of her, its rhythm never faltering, never varying, the vibrations consistent and unyielding. She couldn't quite come down, couldn't move the stimulation away like she always did when her climax became too intense, and was forced instead to ride out wave after wave of inescapable pleasure. Her fingers dug into the stiff leather of the saddle, her pussy clenching endlessly, clit throbbing in overstimulation as she came again, another climax wracking her shuddering body.

She had to turn off the machine. She scrabbled beneath her, flailing for the switches with hands that wouldn't stop shaking, and shut everything down. The machine stopped at last, components freezing in place. Astrid couldn't climb off at first, all her muscles trembling. Finally, she was steady enough to shift and dismount.

Astrid collapsed onto her stool, legs wobbling, waiting to recover completely before attempting to stand up again. Hell's bells, that was a wicked machine. With a damp cloth, she meticulously wiped down the components and the leather. Then, she added necessary modifications to her to-do list. Maybe she would come back on Saturday to complete them and give this device another try.

17

———

Eli whistled to himself as he walked through the light rain on Saturday night, heading to the workshop. In the past two days, he'd managed to put Astrid mostly out of his mind, turn a decent profit in the shop, and even plan for a few improvements on the machine. He and Astrid were scheduled to meet up the next morning, but he wanted to get started ahead of time. It was easier to focus when she wasn't next to him, smelling sweet and desirable.

Shouldering his bag, he let himself into the building and headed down the dark stairway. With any luck, he could finish up his work within the next hour or two. He turned the key in the downstairs lock and walked into their flat.

Strangely, the lights were already on. There was Astrid's cloak on the coat rack, and the muffled whine of the machine echoed from the other room. She must have had the same idea he did, to come in a day early and get some work done on her own. She would certainly be surprised to see him.

The sight of the workshop stopped him dead in the doorway, a current of shock running through his body like electricity. Astrid balanced on the worktable, straddling their machine, which was clearly fucking her without mercy. With her head thrown back, eyes closed, lips parted, she was illuminated like a goddess in the lamplight. Her skirt had ridden up her thighs, and she dug her fingernails into that tender skin with each rocking motion of her hips.

Eli stood frozen, unable to look away from the incredible spectacle of Astrid riding the machine. Oblivious to his presence, she moved and arched in her pleasure, forcing her clit down onto the vibrating ridge and moaning with the contact. His cock hardened in a moment, straining against the buttons of his trousers. In all his time with women, he had never seen this kind of uninhibited wildness. This was an effortless erotic show intended for no audience. An unintentional voyeur, he'd stumbled into this private moment, and this breathtaking sight would be forever seared into his mind each time he closed his eyes.

She hadn't seen him. He could take his coat and go, never mention any of this, meet her in that same workshop the next morning as planned and pretend like nothing happened. At night, when he took his cock in hand, he could remember the look on her face and the heavy scent of sex hanging in the room. There were surely many reasons to leave. Professionalism, probably, or…or…not wanting to get involved with her for some reason? The details were foggy, and his erection begged for more, twitching with no contact whatsoever. When she came, it was going to drive him over the edge, right here, without even touching himself.

As he stood rooted to the spot, his bag of tools slipped down off his shoulder and crashed to the floor.

Astrid's head whipped around, her mouth falling open.

"Eli! Shit!" She slapped around at the base of the machine, searching for the levers, her face and neck crimson. "Oh, God...fuck...where is that fucking switch?"

He was at her side in a moment. Without thinking, he took her face in his hands and drew her lips down to his.

Her hands fluttered for a moment on the edge of the machine before sliding to his shoulders. Her mouth trembled then opened with a desperate sound as she shifted slightly to kiss him back. When he moved one hand down her back, her hips rocked beneath his touch, the machine still running beneath her.

Astrid broke the kiss. "Eli, God—" She threw her head back and shivered, a broken cry slipping from her lips. "It's too much..."

Eli buried his face into the soft skin of her neck and inhaled, overwhelmed and trembling. "Christ, Astrid, I just want to throw you down and fuck you. Do you know that?"

She clutched at the back of his head with her hand, holding his lips against her neck, fingernails digging in as if trying to keep her composure. "Do you want to watch me come? Is that—is that what you want?" As she spoke, she couldn't help moaning as the machine continued to fuck her.

Yes, he wanted that, but he wanted to do more than watch. His throbbing cock was making it difficult to think. "I want to *make* you come. I want to split you open." Still nibbling down her neck, he pressed her hips forward with his hand on the small of her back, driving her clit hard into the vibrator. She cried out, jerking in surprise. "Tell me you want that."

"Yes! Fuck, yes. God, Eli, please, anything, just—just make me come."

He was already unbuttoning his trousers as he switched off

the machine, spinning each dial and lever, bringing the gears to a shuddering halt. Astrid's body sagged, still quivering with unsatisfied pleasure. Before Eli could think twice about it, he lifted her off the machine and set her down on the edge of the worktable. Stepping between her spread knees, he slid forward into her warmth. Her quim trembled around his shaft, tight and slick as he drove all the way in.

Astrid gasped, wrapping her legs around his hips to pull him in even deeper, her hands gripping the back of his shirt. She buried her face in his neck and clutched his back as he began thrusting into her, moaning into his skin, crying out his name and begging him to fuck her.

He could barely keep control. His whole mind was fogged, the world dissolving except for her hot, tight pussy, her breasts pressed against his chest through the tightness of her corset, her breath on his neck, her fingernails digging into his back. He sucked and bit at her ear, her jaw, desperate to taste her as he thrust harder and faster into her warmth. Grabbing the side of his head, she pulled his face to hers, devouring his lips and tongue. He swallowed her desperate sounds, struggling not to come, to hold off his satisfaction for hers.

"Astrid, touch yourself," he begged against her lips.

She leaned back onto the worktable and reached between them to the place where they were joined, finding her clit with slim, nimble fingers. At the contact, her muscles tightened around him, making him cry out. Leaning back even farther, she propped herself up on one arm as the other rubbed her bud. He gritted his teeth, struggling to keep his orgasm at bay, wanting to watch her come. He forced himself to slow down, drawing back most of the way before pushing in again. With each thrust, she rubbed harder and faster, biting her lip, her expression lost in the throes of need.

She was quivering around him now, fluttering at the edge of her climax. Her face and neck were flushed, whole body trembling. That was it. Right there...just a little more. He needed to see this, needed to watch her fall apart. *"Please, Astrid, come for me."*

At his words, she arched back, her pussy clutching at his cock so tightly, he bit his lip to keep from bursting right then. Then she curled forward, legs squeezing his hips like a vise, crying out in bliss. Letting himself go, he began to drive into her, over and over again, harder and faster, hips jerking forward uncontrollably. At the last possible moment, he pulled out, his climax tearing through him and nearly buckling his knees. He rode out the waves of pleasure, emptying himself into his fist as he gripped her hip with his other hand.

When at last he was spent, Eli sank down onto the bench, dizzy and panting, as rational thought came crashing back to him. God, what had he done?

Astrid slid off the table and settled beside him on the bench. She didn't say anything, hands resting on her thighs, her breathing finally calming. He didn't want to talk about this. Trying to gather his thoughts, he got up and began cleaning up with a cloth. Taking direction from him, Astrid did the same, wiping down the machine.

When there was nothing else to clean, Eli stood helpless, his feet leaden, unsure what to say. Astrid faced him from several feet away. Her face was flushed, short hair wild from their frantic sex, lips swollen from his kisses. Her stance challenged him, legs slightly apart with her hands on her hips.

What was it about her that made him unable to think straight?

Before he could frame a question or statement, Astrid gave him a half smile. "I suppose you caught me."

He struggled to be articulate. "How—how long have you been using the machine?"

She rubbed the back of her neck with one hand, ducking her head, somehow shy even after that shameless display. "A couple of days. I've been coming in here at night. And...*coming* in here at night." Her relaxed smile took some of his tension away. This didn't have to be the end of their working relationship. They both just got carried away.

"I'm sorry for what happened there." Eli leaned against the worktable, reminded suddenly of how she'd looked sitting on it while he fucked her not ten minutes earlier. "We shouldn't have done that."

Her smile faded. "If you say so. But I wasn't the one spying."

"I was not spying! I came down here to make some modifications. I wanted to make the switches easier to reach, for one thing." He walked past her to examine the machine, more so he didn't have to look at that disappointed expression on her face. Each time he looked at her, he wanted to take her into his arms again. But if he let himself have that, if he got too close to her, it would hurt all the more when she ultimately left him. "I think maybe we should take a few more days apart. I don't want this kind of thing to happen again." That was a blatant lie, of course, and she probably knew it. He wanted this kind of thing to happen over and over again, but it wasn't prudent.

"Well, maybe you should keep your dick in your pants, then."

The anger in her voice made him turn. She folded her arms across her chest, like she was putting up a wall between them. "I mean it. If you don't want to have sex with me, don't have sex with me. But this 'yes, yes, yes' followed by 'no, no, no' isn't fair to either of us."

"I'm sorry." He ran a hand through his hair. Now she thought he didn't want her, and he had to try and explain. "It's not that I don't want you. Clearly. But you and me? We're such different people, Astrid." That was an understatement. He was boring, predictable, professional, and she was wild, brave and creative.

Her jaw tightened almost imperceptibly. "Oh. Okay, I get it." She looked off to the side. "Sure. Let's take a few days off. Wednesday? The usual time?"

"All right." Her annoyance unsettled him, but he didn't know how to address it. Maybe by Wednesday, they could get back to normal.

18

When the door buzzer went off, Astrid jumped and dropped her spanner and the vibrator she'd been building. She wasn't expecting guests. Clients usually sent her a message first. With Josian out of town, it was unusual for anyone to drop by.

The woman on the other side of the door was the last person Astrid expected to see. "Cecily?"

In the two years since Astrid had last seen Cecily Lahey, the woman had grown even more beautiful. All soft curves and impossibly long red hair, she wore a peacock-blue skirt that filled the hallway in waves, paired with a frilled tan blouse and a brown leather corset with brass ornamentation. Her face was as lovely as a painting, creamy skin dusted with freckles, mischievous green eyes framed with long, dark lashes —helped along substantially with makeup, of course, and the overall effect was mesmerizing.

"Astrid! I haven't seen you in years. You look simply fantastic." Sweeping into the room, Cecily wrapped her arms around Astrid and pulled her in for a close hug. She smelled fresh and clean, like rosewater, and the scent instantly brought Astrid back several years to the Lahey Emporium, to unsettled days and heady, pleasure-filled nights in Cecily's arms. Astrid stepped backward, escaping the hug and the memories, her throat suddenly dry. Cecily didn't seem to care, though; she looked around the room with bright interest. "Look at this flat! A modern independent woman, yes? Like you always wanted."

"I suppose." Astrid stared as Cecily began to examine everything in the living room: the sofa and parlor chairs, the tables, the paintings on the walls. How fortuitous that she'd been up since six cleaning, trying to quiet her restless mind and unsettled emotions by scrubbing all surfaces with near-fanatical precision. Her flat had never looked nicer.

When Cecily reached the display case, she stopped and smiled, tracing one finger over the bottom frame. "You've done well for yourself, Astrid. I knew you would." She turned to smile at Astrid, who was still trying to make sense of the situation.

"Cecily, why are you here?"

Cecily brushed her ginger curls back over her shoulder. "I heard that you were the woman to see about felicitation devices."

So this was about business, then. "I do still make them. Are these for you? Or for the emporium?"

Cecily smiled. "Some of each, but mostly for the business. My girls need variety in their escapades. I want to purchase some devices they can use on themselves and their clients."

"I mostly design for women. I'm not sure if any of my devices will be right for men." Thinking of men had her thinking of Eli, and she didn't want to do that, not after their complicated encounter last night. "May I get you some tea?"

"Please."

Astrid put the kettle on. "Do you have anything particular in mind?"

Cecily tapped the glass with one perfect oval fingernail. "Open this up. Let's see what you have."

Cecily pored over the merchandise in the display case. She tested each device for its range of vibrations and movements, working through the case one at a time. Eli had examined her products as well, delicate and reverent where Cecily was direct and businesslike. Thinking of Eli made Astrid's heart constrict.

"I hadn't expected you to have quite so many," Cecily said. "Back at the emporium, you'd only created this one." She turned the first model over in her hand, the basic cylindrical vibrator that had launched Astrid's entire business. "Choosing is more difficult than I thought it would be. What do you recommend?"

Astrid's reply was interrupted by the kettle. When she rejoined Cecily at the case, she examined her collection with fresh eyes. She had no idea what a man would like. Eventually, she held up the one that had so fascinated Eli, the device that strapped on to one's hand and turned the fingers into individual vibrators. "This one is called the Always Handy Stimulator and Felicitator. Useful for someone giving a man special attention, I suppose." She attached it to her hand, then switched it on and traced her fingers over Cecily's palm.

"Yes, that's very nice. A bit intimidating to look at, though."

"Best used in the dark, I think." Astrid replaced the device in its case. "Of course, there's always the basic one you remember. Provides constant surface vibration."

Cecily clasped her hands behind her back. "These will do for the average customer, but many of our clients want something a bit more. Do you have anything that would be suitable for the arse?"

Astrid considered. "I haven't designed anything specifically for that purpose, although I imagine some of these items might work…" Her mind raced as she scanned the shelves. "Most of my clients are beginners, and no one has requested that yet, but I imagine it would be easy enough. Do you want me to design something? If you can tell me how it needs to be different than these, I can create a device to suit your needs. Your business's needs." She found a notepad and pen on her desk, which had been denuded of all excess machinery and paraphernalia.

Cecily tapped her lips with a finger and began giving direction as Astrid took note. "It will definitely need a flared base, else it might slip inside and get lost. Wouldn't want to consult a home physician for that sort of removal. Firmness is key, but you've got that figured out in your material construction anyway. Of course it needs to vibrate." She continued perusing the devices. "Make two different ones, one small, one a bit larger. Make the larger one curved, if you can. Good for internal stimulation."

Astrid finished scribbling the specifications in her notes. She wasn't working with Eli until Wednesday, so she had some free time. "I could have this for you by the end of the week, I think."

"That would be lovely. If I like your work, maybe we can work out a more permanent arrangement."

An ongoing contract with the Lahey Emporium would ease her financial burdens substantially. She couldn't count on that, though, until these devices were finished. Astrid looked over her notes. "I've never tried a device like this. I never understood the appeal, personally."

"It's more common than you might think. Quite an erogenous zone." Cecily folded her hands. "I could show you, if you'd like."

Astrid had spent a year with Cecily, a year giving and taking pleasure without emotional entanglements. Eli came to mind again. "I think maybe that's not such a good idea."

Cecily cocked her head to the side, scrutinizing Astrid, a slight smile playing at her lips. "So who is he?"

Ten minutes later, Cecily was nodding sympathetically as Astrid finished her story over tea.

"And we were supposed to be working together today, but he asked to put it off until Wednesday because he needed to clear his head. Says we're 'different people.' I'm sure he means that he's the proper kind of people, and I'm the lowborn kind of people, but I'm certainly not too lowborn for him to bed, right? I just... God, Cecily, I don't understand men. One minute he's holding me in his arms like he never wants me to leave, and the next he doesn't want to get too close."

"Mmm." Cecily sipped her tea, her expression difficult to read. Although enigmatic herself, she'd always been able to see through other people, cut past what they said to what they meant. That was probably what made her business so successful. When Astrid expected her to give advice, though, she remained silent.

Finally, Astrid prompted her. "What do you think?"

Cecily took another sip of tea, slowly, seeming to hold the

flavor in her mouth for a long moment before swallowing. She licked a drop off the corner of her lip, her eyes still perusing Astrid's face. "Does he know that you're falling in love with him?"

Astrid's hand slipped on the cup, spilling tea over the saucer and the sofa, narrowly missing Cecily's beautiful dress. "Oh shit! Shit. I just…" She mopped at the spill with a tea towel. "I don't… Cecily, I'm not…" Even as she denied it, her face flushed warm. She continued to blot at the sofa long after she'd soaked up all the tea, not ready to meet the other woman's eyes yet.

Cecily didn't respond, her expression placid when Astrid finally dared to look up. Falling in love with Eli made no sense whatsoever. It was ridiculous; they'd only been working together a couple of weeks. She was a grown woman, not a lovestruck maid, and they had no real future together, as he'd made abundantly clear the night before. That didn't even bother her, actually, since he was so arrogant and pretentious. All he cared about was his reputation. He didn't really care about her, so it didn't matter what became of him, because she wasn't falling in love with him. She couldn't be falling in love with him.

She was falling in love with him.

Astrid sighed, her body folding in on itself like a house of cards. "Cecily, what am I going to do?"

Cecily stroked gentle circles on her back. "You could always pursue him anyway. Class is such an illusion. If two people love each other, none of that matters. Not anymore. Not like it used to." She smiled warmly. "Sooner or later, he's bound to realize that."

"If he loved me, perhaps. Which he doesn't." Astrid leaned

her head on the back of the sofa, staring up at the ceiling. This whole situation was ridiculous, even laughable. So why did she feel so much like crying?

Cecily set her cup and saucer aside on the table. "If you're not going to pursue him, then you need to forget him. Distance yourself."

"That's not so easy. We're working together on this World's Fair project." She hadn't told Cecily the nature of the device, only that it was a joint venture.

"Then see him as little as possible. Work together when you have to, but separate yourself otherwise. Focus on your business, your hobbies. Find a distraction to fill your mind and your bed. When the World's Fair is over, you probably don't ever need to see this man again." Cecily patted Astrid's knee. "You're still young. You'll move on, like we all do."

"I suppose."

Cecily's hand wandered up Astrid's thigh, stroking her leg through the fabric of her skirt. Astrid focused on the contact, the gentle touch, the promise underlying that contact. "I can distract you, Astrid," she said softly.

Astrid let herself look into Cecily's green eyes. She had never been in love with Cecily, nor Cecily with her. Their time together had been carefree and pleasurable, a welcome respite from the stresses of life, two friends taking refuge in each other's arms. She could experience that again. They could exchange satisfaction without it meaning anything else. Perhaps she could forget about Eli in someone else's touch.

"I don't know, Cecily. Things are so complicated right now." Her arguments against this arrangement seemed weak, all centered around Eli, Eli who was probably not thinking of her at all.

"Then let's keep it simple." Cecily glided closer to her on the sofa, brought her hand up to stroke the back of Astrid's head. "I've missed you, Astrid. Being here with you reminds me of what lovely nights we used to have." Her touch was gentle, drifting from Astrid's hair to the side of her face. "I can help you forget him."

It was easy, then, to close her eyes to Cecily's sweet kiss. It had always been easy. Those kisses were familiar, half forgotten in the intervening years, Cecily's lips pliant and soft. She tasted lovely, like the peppermint tea. Before Astrid knew exactly what she was doing, she had her arms around Cecily, one hand tangled in that long, glorious hair.

It wasn't the same, of course. Cecily's face felt smooth against her neck when she began kissing her there, no trace of a beard or stubble. Cecily's touch was delicate against Astrid's cheek, then her collarbone, then her breast.

Different didn't mean worse, though. In the bedroom, Cecily went to work on Astrid's clothing, thin fingers deftly undressing her as they continued to kiss. Astrid was dizzy, the kind of dizzy she wanted to be, the kind that washed away thoughts. Within moments, she lay naked on the bed. Wanting to reciprocate, she reached up to fumble for the fastenings on Cecily's corset. Cecily lowered her lips to Astrid's breast, and Astrid's hands fell bonelessly away from their task.

Although they hadn't been lovers in nearly two years, Cecily still remembered what Astrid liked, using her teeth, biting and pinching each nipple before laving them with her tongue. Each stroke sent a direct jolt to Astrid's clit. The long locks of Cecily's hair tumbled across Astrid's stomach, soft and silky beneath her fingers, leaving tickling trails of sensation as Cecily kissed her way down to the soft curls at the juncture of Astrid's thighs.

She blew a cool breath of air across the hot folds, and Astrid gasped. She'd become so sensitive so quickly. This was good. She could forget like this. She could lose herself in the feeling. One long, slow drag of Cecily's tongue, and her mind went completely blank except for the exquisite wave of pleasure running up through her body.

"That's right. Do you like that?" Cecily looked up at her, smiling, before lowering her lips to Astrid's skin once more.

Cecily approached sex with a single-minded focus that made sense, given her profession. She started with long licks and then began sucking directly on Astrid's clit, drawing it between her teeth until her lover was moaning shamelessly. The attention was too intense, her feelings sharp and bordering on pain, but Astrid yielded to all of it as she was dragged over the edge into orgasm. The climax was fast, intense and brutal, a great shuddering rush that crashed through her and then melted away, leaving Astrid breathless and spent.

"There, that helps, right?" Cecily smiled, shedding her own clothing with methodical precision. "The first one really takes the edge off."

Astrid watched Cecily undress, a strange disembodied sense settling over her. The orgasm had been good, of course; Cecily was an expert, but it wasn't the same as Eli's passionate, desperate fucking from last night or the deliberate, patient way he had used his mouth on her their first time together. Cecily always sought climax, her partner's and her own, without delay. No matter how many times they slept together, it never got personal, just a task to be completed:

mutually beneficial, but never earth-shattering. The thought made Astrid feel oddly lonely for Cecily and brought her own loneliness into sharp relief. She put it aside and tried to focus on the moment.

Cecily dropped the last of her underthings on the floor and caught Astrid's gaze. If she had any inkling about her lover's thoughts, she didn't comment; she simply leaned over and took Astrid's mouth under hers again. Astrid ran her fingers down Cecily's back, loving the feeling of soft skin beneath her hands. Then she reached between them, cupping Cecily's voluptuous breasts, rubbing the nipples with her thumbs. Cecily sighed in pleasure, smiling as she leaned up on her elbows.

"That's nice, you know that?" She dropped a light kiss on Astrid's lips, then sat up and opened the nightstand drawer. "Ahh, here we go."

Cecily poked around in the drawer, choosing between items. When Astrid leaned up to see, a gentle hand pushed her back to the bed. "Now, now. You lie back and let me take care of this." Cecily brushed her hair back behind her shoulder and gave Astrid a warm smile. In a moment, she scooted back between her lover's legs.

Her thumb found Astrid's clit with ease, rubbing in firm, practiced circles. With her knees falling out to the sides, Astrid felt completely exposed, but she loved that feeling. She closed her eyes.

Cecily's other hand brushed gently against Astrid's arse, her fingers that felt warm and slippery with lubrication that she must have taken from the bedside drawer. "This all right?" Cecily asked, and Astrid nodded without opening her eyes.

"I'm not saying I'll like it," Astrid warned.

Cecily chuckled. "If you don't like it, I'll stop."

When one finger pressed inside, Astrid sucked in a breath, eyes opening in shock. That was unusual, but not unpleasant, and with the continuous stimulation of her clit, unusual soon turned to something lovely. Cecily stroked her finger in and out. Astrid felt warm and shivery at the same time, ripples of sensation beginning to run through her.

"Should I stop?" Cecily asked.

"*God*, no." Astrid could come just from this, tension building ever higher. Right when she thought her climax was inevitable, Cecily stopped and left her panting.

Before she could complain, or do anything but moan, Cecily's finger was replaced by something else, a cold shock of metal that made her arch up off the bed. After a moment, it began vibrating. "Oh, fuck..." was all she could manage as the shaft moved back and forth. That feeling overwhelmed all conscious thought and action, and all she wanted was to come. After a moment, a hard, firm object slid deep into her pussy and up against her clit. She clenched reflexively, tightening around the objects filling both holes, gasping and unable to get enough air as that device, too, began vibrating. Her orgasm crashed over her immediately, tearing through her in rolling waves, white-hot and intense. Nothing existed but her body and the throbbing between her legs.

She came down slowly, consciousness returning bit by bit as the pleasure subsided. The bone-deep satisfaction of climax settled over her. Cecily slowly removed the devices and began wiping them down with a cloth, a satisfied smile on her lips. "Are you back with us now?"

"Mmm." Astrid pushed up to a sitting position on the bed. "Thank you."

"Happy to oblige. You really like this one, don't you?" Cecily was holding the sleek wooden one she'd used on Astrid, studying the external clit nub.

"My current favorite."

Astrid sat up to kiss Cecily, the best way she knew to show her appreciation. She carefully guided Cecily down onto her back. "Do you want to try it?"

"Please."

By the way Cecily sighed and arched when Astrid slid the shaft inside her, this wouldn't take long. It never did; Cecily reached climax more easily than any man Astrid had taken to bed. Astrid didn't mind: while she enjoyed sex, and definitely enjoyed sex with Cecily, Eli kept slipping back into her mind. She tried to focus on the task at hand. Cecily's body was easy to read—she flushed across her neck and chest, nipples tightening, and her hips began rocking against Astrid's hand. Time to go faster, harder; she loved the little noises Cecily made when she got close. Cecily arched up off the bed and came, her beautiful red hair spilling across the pillow as she tossed her head. Then she relaxed, limp and spent, softening into the bed as she lay back down.

After setting the device aside, Astrid curled up next to Cecily. The other woman pulled her close, an embrace that was comforting but not romantic. Astrid breathed in the scent of rosewater and tried to relax, tried not to remember the way Eli had curled around her in the dark, his touch protective and intimate. In Cecily's embrace, maybe she could learn to forget.

19

———

Although he'd agreed to meet Astrid at ten, Eli arrived at their workshop shortly after nine. After what had happened the previous week, he wanted time to get his bearings before she arrived.

Whatever peace of mind he'd achieved by staying away from her evaporated when he walked inside and saw the room exactly as they'd left it Saturday night. Memories of that night, of Astrid, had haunted him relentlessly in the intervening days. He'd begun to entertain ridiculous ideas, like courting her despite their different personalities and the certainty of heartbreak. Even knowing what a bad idea it was for them to be together, if she propositioned him again, he wasn't sure he'd say no.

Best not to dwell on that line of thought. The brass piping he'd ordered had been delivered, so he pulled out the welding gear and began building the frame, putting the distracting thoughts out of his mind.

"Hi."

Eli cut the torch and pushed up his welding goggles at the

sound of her voice behind him. He had no idea how long she'd been standing there. "Hi."

Something had changed in Astrid in the past few days. Her expression was guarded, her jaw set. She didn't look mad, exactly, but the reckless playfulness of the past few weeks had all but vanished. "Working on the frame, then?" she asked.

He nodded to the partially built structure of piping. "I ordered the pipes on Monday, and they were waiting for me when I got here. I thought I could work on the framing, and you could build the devices for the final model." When he gestured to the machine prototype, he immediately wished he hadn't. She followed his gaze to the saddle. Surely they were both thinking the same thing. Eli cleared his throat. "Unless you want to take them out of the prototype and put them in the finished model."

She walked over to the prototype and examined the devices, God help him, handling them as if they were nothing but tools. After a moment's consideration, she shook her head. "No, I think I want to keep this intact. I can build another set. We're still ten days out from the Judges' Viewing, and I have time."

Without saying anything else to him, she gathered some equipment and sat down at the other workbench.

The tension between them had been challenging before, but this silence was more awkward than he had anticipated. Worst of all, Astrid didn't seem bothered by it. Every time he looked over at her, she was bent over her work, assembling components with unbroken focus. Somehow, she remained dispassionate while he jumped and looked over each time she moved.

Not until they stopped for lunch did she say anything

further to him at all. They sat side by side on the workbench, chewing in silence, when she finally spoke through a mouthful of sandwich.

"What did you say?" he asked.

She swallowed. "It has to have a name."

He followed her line of sight to the machine prototype on the worktable. Right, a name for the machine. At least she was talking to him. "It oscillates."

"And it's a felicitator, like the rest of my devices." She chewed another bite then swallowed, still staring at the machine. "It's an oscillating felicitator."

"Is that what we call it, then? The Oscillating Felicitator?"

Astrid looked down into her sandwich. Her expression was pensive, brows knit, teeth nibbling her bottom lip. She couldn't know how much that expression made him want to kiss her. She couldn't be doing it on purpose. She hadn't touched him at all that day, not even an accidental brush past him while getting a tool off the shelf.

"We should both get credit. I say we call it the Bailey-Rutledge Oscillating Felicitator." She looked over at him. "What do you think?"

He rubbed his beard. "That's a mouthful. Can I call it the Ossy?"

"If that makes you happy." Astrid took another bite of sandwich, and their conversation was over.

By the time Eli finished the frame and the gear assembly, his eyes were bleary. Astrid continued to work at her bench, peering through the magnifying lens at the tiny components she was handling. She showed no signs of stopping.

"It's after five." Eli began packing up his own tools,

relieved to have an excuse to leave the uncomfortable environment. "I'm going to call it a day."

At first it looked like she hadn't heard him, but then she set the tools down and stretched, arching her back like a cat. She arched like that when she came, too, and his cock stirred in his trousers. He could take a moment to broach the subject of their last encounter, just to clear the air...but no, not with that disinterested way she was packing up her tools. He'd asked for distance, and she was giving it to him.

As she turned to leave, he called after her. "Tomorrow? Same time?"

"All right." She moved past him and left.

Eli gathered his thoughts as he gathered his tools, aware of the emptiness of their small workshop without Astrid there. He should have said more to her. Maybe he would take the long way home, the way that passed by her flat. If he saw her, perhaps he could clear things up between them in a neutral space. There was no reason they couldn't be friends.

The night was warm and uncharacteristically dry, the sun just fading below the skyline. He followed the same route Astrid had taken the night he walked home with her, turning down her street, remembering the anticipation and anxiety he'd felt as they approached her flat. Tonight, the same mix of emotions ran through him.

When he turned the corner, he caught sight of her walking a few blocks ahead of him. She approached the front steps of her building, but the door opened before she could use her key. From this distance, in the fading light, he could barely make out the smile on her face. Then a woman stepped out of the front entryway and kissed Astrid on the mouth.

A trickle of ice ran down his spine, stopping him where he

stood in the shadow of a tenement building. He watched, unable to look away, as Astrid kissed the woman back, reaching one hand up to cup her lover's cheek before following her back inside. The cold lingered long after Astrid had closed the door and left him alone on the deserted street in the gathering twilight, long after his own silent walk home.

20

————

Maybe today it would be easier to be cold to Eli. Astrid took a moment to compose her thoughts outside the door to their workshop flat, prepared to find him already inside. She wanted to have the right expression when she saw him. It had taken almost all her effort to cultivate aloofness with him yesterday, but maybe today she wouldn't struggle so much.

His back was to her when she entered the workshop itself. As soon as she greeted him, his shoulders tensed. That might be because of her or because he had turned on the hammer machine. Either way, he didn't turn around, and she settled down to work, the hammering a constant drone that eventually faded into the background.

Deep into her own work, she didn't notice right away when the room went silent. She set down her machinery and turned to see what Eli was doing. He was watching her, holding the brass saddle in hand, mouth slightly agape like he was unsure what to do or say.

Astrid surveyed the situation. "Are you all right?"

"I was just trying to figure out how far along you were with the devices. I'm nearly ready to fit the saddle."

"Did you think about asking me?" Maybe she was supposed to read minds now. Or maybe she was supposed to figure out on her own that he was waiting for her.

"I thought about it, but I didn't want to disturb you." While his words were thoughtful, his tone was clearly annoyed, his body language tense.

Whatever had gotten into him, she didn't want to deal with his problems. "I'm nearly finished with the clit vibrator, but I haven't started on the shaft yet. I can probably finish that by the end of the day. Can you do anything in the meantime?"

"I suppose I can finish the gear work."

"Well, do that then."

Eli seemed to want to say something to her, but after a moment of his ambivalence, she turned back to the worktable. She had her own tasks to finish.

Her morning was punctuated by a few other interruptions like that one. Eli would ask her some inane question, pause inordinately long after her answer, then return to work. Finally, after the third such occurrence, she put her work down with more force than usual and turned back to face him.

"Eli, is there something you want to say to me? Or are you just going to keep interrupting me and then staring at me all day?"

His jaw hardened, eyes narrowing. He licked his upper lip, pausing before answering her. "All right, yes, there's something I want to say to you. How long have you been seeing that woman?"

Astrid's body heated, sudden anger blooming in her stomach. So that's what this was all about. He saw her with Cecily somehow, and now he wanted to hear the specifics. She fought to keep her voice level. "Follow me home last night?"

"It wasn't like that. I was hoping to see you and get a chance to clear things up between us." His eyes flicked sideways to the machine prototype, sitting on the worktable like a manifestation of the elephant in the room.

"There's nothing to clear up." Astrid's throat had grown tight. He must have seen Cecily meet her at the door. "What's happening between Cecily and me is none of your business."

"Cecily?" Oh, damn, he probably would remember the name from dinner. He leaned back against the workbench. "As in Cecily Lahey?"

"So what if it is?" Astrid scooted up from the bench to sit on the table, disliking the feeling of sitting below Eli's eye level.

"So she…she…?" Eli waved his hand, searching for the right word.

"She what? Runs a brothel? Buys my felicitation devices? Took me in when I needed help?" Astrid felt herself growing louder and had to work to lower her volume. "She's a good friend I can rely on."

"It seems like she's more than a friend, from what I saw last night." Eli folded his arms, his jaw set.

Astrid's mouth fell open, her racing heartbeat making it difficult to think. His rudeness, his presumption, was staggering. He had no right to ask about her personal life. "What are you implying, Eli? That Cecily and I are sleeping together?"

"Well, are you?"

"So what if we are? I don't think you have a say in who I sleep with." When he looked at her, jealousy flared in his eyes, and that made her even angrier. "What business is it of yours, anyway? Last time I checked, we were 'such different people.' Sleeping together was 'a bad idea.' Has any of that changed?"

Eli's mouth opened and closed a few times, but Astrid didn't want to wait for him to come up with an answer.

"I can't believe you. Yes, I'm sleeping with Cecily. I like her. I like having sex with her. I'm not in a relationship with her, as you so quickly assumed." She got to her feet, fists clenching. "Do you know why I like her? Because she doesn't look down on me for who I am and what I do." When Eli went to speak, she raised her hand. "Don't you dare say you don't judge me. I see the way you look at me sometimes, when you think I'm not looking." Angry tears prickled at the corners of her eyes, and she blinked them back. She was not going to cry.

Expecting that Eli might attempt to pacify her or apologize, she was ready to shoot down his kindness. Instead, he responded with the same intensity.

"So *I'm* judging *you*?" The anger in his voice made her step back in surprise, bumping into the worktable. "You took one look at me and thought you had me completely figured out. You refuse to believe that anyone else could have suffered as much as you have. You won't ask for help, even when you need it. You're stubborn as hell and too independent for your own good, and you won't admit that you need me in this. You need this build, and I'm as much a part of it as you are."

Astrid gave a short, mirthless laugh. "All right, so I want to win the World's Fair, and thanks to this misogynistic perversion of a trade commission, I have to team up with you. You've got me. Clearly I'm a heartless bitch because I didn't want to give out my idea to the first bloke who came along."

Eli shook his head. "I don't believe you. I am doing more

than my share in this partnership and you know it. And God forbid I show some surprise that you're hiding Cecily from me! If you really don't care what I think, why not say something about her earlier?"

How dare he! Astrid tensed like a coiled spring, her fingernails digging sharp pinpricks of pain into her palms. "So now I have to report to you? What I do in my bedroom is none of your business. You do not get any say about who I do and do not have sex with, because you and I are not in a relationship."

Eli stepped forward, entering her space in a deliberate way that would have made her back up if she weren't already pressed against the table. She had never fully appreciated his height until he stood towering over her, a solid wall of man. The air between them crackled with electricity, and she suddenly struggled to breathe, her body responding to his proximity in ways she couldn't control.

When he met her eyes, her annoyance dissolved in the wake of desire. His voice grew husky, his words rumbling against her skin as he pressed himself against her. "I think what happens in your bedroom became my business once you invited me into it."

She couldn't repress a shiver as he cupped the back of her head. "Oh, you think so, do you?" Her voice was barely audible in her own ears, shaky with forced bravado and undeniable need.

"Yes, I do." He dragged her mouth to his.

God, he shouldn't be able to kiss her like this, his mouth insistent, his tongue twining with hers. If he didn't grab her arse and lift her leg up over his hip, she wouldn't be tangling her hands in his hair. If he didn't press himself between her thighs, she wouldn't be thrusting up against his cock.

Eli brushed her throat with his lips then his teeth, nibbling his way down the ribbon of sensitive flesh. "Tell me you don't want this." He reached up beneath her skirt and groaned as his fingers slipped through her wet folds between her legs. At the first touch of his fingertips, her knees weakened, and she threw her head back with a moan. "That's right," he said against her neck, holding her immobile in his strong arms. "You want me to fuck you again, don't you?"

Struggling for her footing, she pulled back slightly, still pressed against the table, and reached around to the front of his trousers to cup his erection. To her satisfaction, he hissed in a breath, his hand slipping away from her to steady himself on the table. "Clearly I'm not the only one." She gripped his shaft through the fabric of his trousers, and his mouth fell open. "What's the matter? Bad idea not seeming so bad anymore?"

Eli met her eyes, a half smile flicking across his lips. "Cecily doesn't have one of those, does she?"

Astrid smirked, releasing him. "On the contrary, we have a whole drawer full of them."

"You think you're funny, don't you?" With a growl, Eli picked her up and carried her bodily out of the workshop, into the living room. "You don't have one like this, I promise."

Astrid held on, wrapping her legs around his hips, pressing openmouthed kisses to his neck. "You mean attached to a pompous fuckwit?"

Eli dropped her lengthwise onto the sofa and immediately climbed over her, bracing himself on his elbows as he began kissing his way down her chest. When he reached the neckline of her blouse, he lingered there and began unfastening the metal busk of her corset. "Better a pompous fuckwit than a self-righteous bitch, wouldn't you say?"

With his lips caressing the tops of her breasts, Astrid couldn't think of something mean to say. He pressed one leg right between her thighs, forcing her knees apart as he finally finished unhooking her corset and tossed it aside. "I am not a self-righteous…ohh…" Her retort faded as he closed his lips over her nipple, sucking through the fabric of her sheer blouse. The rough, wet cloth against her sensitive flesh made her skin tingle, her body burning up with heat. When he switched to the other breast, the cool air brushing the wet fabric sent a shiver through her. She squirmed against his thigh, seeking some kind of relief from the sudden ache between her legs.

Eli lifted his head, smiling as if he thought he'd won, and drove his leg more firmly against her. "Hmm? What was that? You're not what?"

She couldn't find a coherent thought, especially when he began twisting her nipples between his fingers. Her eyes slammed shut as she sank back against the sofa cushions, spikes of pleasure mingling with pain as he pinched harder. Eli began sucking on her neck again, his mouth finding the point where her pulse fluttered beneath the skin. The sound that escaped her lips was indecent, low and husky and wanton; his cock throbbed against her thigh at the sound.

Astrid opened her eyes and pushed him away from her. Before he could pull her back in, she climbed over his lap and straddled his hips, hiking her skirt up. "You're a complete arse, Eli Rutledge." As she spoke, she pulled his shirt from his trousers and began unbuttoning it with a ferocious carelessness. "You can't keep your hands off me." After tugging his shirt off, she yanked his undershirt over his head, revealing his bare skin. She raked her fingers down his chest, deliberately scraping his nipples, eliciting a low groan. He watched her motions, his eyes dark and liquid in the dim light of the flickering lamps. She curled her fingers in the crinkly hair on his chest, loving the rough texture, the way it rubbed against the tender peaks of her breasts when she leaned forward to kiss him.

Eli's hands went to her hips, holding her in place, and he thrust against her. The rough wool fabric of his trousers pressed just so against her clit, sending a spike of pleasure through her. "Is it like this with Cecily? Does she make you feel this way?"

His jealousy, the repressed anger in his eyes, made her burn with a mixture of irritation and arousal. "Maybe." He didn't need to know the truth, that Cecily was sweet but distant, that sex with her was barely more emotional than fucking a felicitation device. Astrid didn't want to give him the satisfaction of knowing how much she wanted this breathless passion and intensity. Reaching down between them, she found Eli's trouser buttons, deftly flicking each one open, making sure to brush against his straining erection as she did so. "Is that what you want? Do you want me to tell you how she brings me off with her tongue?" Sitting back farther on his thighs, she tugged at his trousers until he lifted his hips and let her slide them all he way off. She wrapped her hand around his thick cock, enjoying the way his eyes fell half closed when she did so. "Or do you want to admit that you don't want to share?"

The way she stroked his shaft was leaving him speechless.

When she began rubbing her thumb over the tip, his head fell back against the sofa, his fingers digging into the cushions. "God, *Astrid.*" He said her name like both a curse and a prayer.

Watching him come undone was hypnotizing, and she wanted more; she wanted him completely at her mercy. She shouldn't be the one to feel powerless all the time. Sliding down off the sofa, she knelt between his legs. Right when he noticed she had moved, just as he opened his eyes, she leaned forward and closed her lips over the head of his erection.

His hips stilled instantly, body motionless as if he couldn't believe what was happening. When she slid her lips down to the base, taking him all the way inside her mouth, he groaned. That helpless, throaty sound was so hot, her clit throbbed just from hearing him.

His hips remained frozen in place, his hands clenched tightly at his sides, clearly fighting the sensations. That wouldn't do at all. She wanted to see him helpless and begging. She focused on just the head, tonguing the slit, grasping the shaft with one hand. He twitched with each stroke of her tongue. She peered up through her lashes to see him gritting his teeth, arousal mingling with determination on his expression. This was a battle, then, and she was going to make him fall apart.

Slipping one hand down between her legs, she slid a finger inside herself, coating it with her slickness, before reaching up behind his sac to brush his puckered hole.

Eli's hips jerked forward, thrusting his cock forward into her mouth, and he cried out once in surprise before pulling back. Astrid let his dick slide out from between her lips and met his eyes, her slick finger still tracing small circles on his hole. His head fell back, eyes closing.

"Do you like this?" she asked. He obviously liked it, and she was clearly driving him out of his mind, but she wanted to hear it. His hips thrust slightly into empty air, cock twitching with his heartbeat. She pressed a bit harder, the tip of her finger threatening to slip inside, and he let out a low, guttural noise that made her drip with arousal.

"Tell me you want this." Bending down, she licked the tip of his cock again, and it bobbed against her lips. "Do you want my finger in you?"

He nodded, biting his lower lip. That was good enough for now. She took him in her mouth again as she slid her finger slowly inside.

"Oh, fuck…fuck…fuck…God, yes." His swearing became less coherent when she curled her finger. He tangled one hand in her hair, gripping but not restraining, as he began to thrust into her mouth. He tasted so good, salty and a bit tangy, the taste of a man falling apart. As she continued, he began to breathe more erratically, trembling as he reached the edge. The power of her position made her body thrum with heat.

"Christ, Astrid. You've got…you've got to…"

She ran her tongue from base to tip. "Got to what?"

"You've got to stop, or I can't…can't hold on."

"No. I want to make you come."

She took him into her mouth again, sucking hard as she pressed her fingertip against the perfect spot inside him. When he came, he cried out her name, bucking his hips helplessly and emptying himself into her mouth. She drank him down, sucking until he began to grow soft. Then she withdrew her finger and sat back on her heels to look up at him.

Head lolling back against the sofa, Eli was a picture of distraction: disheveled, hair askew, panting and sweaty in his half-unclothed disarray. She had taken him to that point. After a moment, though, he dragged her back up onto his lap, biting down gently on her neck in a way that made her bones go wobbly. Somehow, his cock twitched between them. "Already?" she asked.

"Give me a few minutes, but I'm not that old." He traced her jaw. "I want you."

"I know you want me." Astrid slid off him, escaping his grasp, then began unfastening her boots. "How do you feel about me?"

"I feel like I want you." Eli shucked his own shoes then the rest of his clothes as she tossed off hers as well. When she climbed back onto his lap, straddling his thighs, he ran his hands up her back and pulled her flush against his chest. His heart beat a rhythm against hers. He slipped a hand between them, finding her clit, and she dug her nails into his shoulders at the rush. "Feels like you want me too." He pressed two fingers up into her, slid them deep, and curled them in a way that made sparks erupt behind her eyes. "Tell me you want me."

"God, you're such an arse." She pressed her mouth to his, riding his fingers like she wanted to ride his cock, which was steadily coming to full attention again between them.

He stilled her hips with his free hand, holding her steady while he curled his fingers inside her and rubbed hard. His thumb brushed her clit, and the combined stimulation made her break their kiss to gasp for air. She couldn't squirm away, just like the beautiful helplessness of riding the Ossy. She'd never been with a man who could play her body so well, hitting the exact right spots and driving her to the edge so quickly. Before she could quiver apart just from his fingers, he pulled her down onto his cock.

Astrid sighed against Eli's lips, his hard length throbbing inside her. For a moment, she stayed like that, savoring his hot flesh against hers, her muscles tensing around him. When she lifted her hips and pressed down again, the pleasure made her eyes fall closed. Oh, that was good. She began to ride him, angling her hips so he hit the right spot with each stroke. She could focus entirely on the physical, could push emotions aside.

"Look at me."

At the sound of Eli's voice, Astrid made herself open her eyes to meet his. God, his eyes. They were wide, the pupils dark, lust and need written across his expression. With each thrust of her hips, his eyelids fluttered, his jaw going slack. Then he slipped his hand between them again and began rubbing her clit. Her hands tightened on his shoulders as sparks sizzled along her nerves.

"That's right." He continued to rub in steady circles, staying with her as she rocked her hips against him and coherent thought slipped away. The slow climb was beginning, driving her higher with each stroke, her movements becoming erratic.

"I want to feel you come." Eli began thrusting upward now, his touch on her clit never wavering. He was close too, the muscles in his neck tense with effort of holding back, but he didn't break eye contact. Somehow, this was the most intimate they'd been; she was seeing him plainly for the first time, unable to close out the raw emotion in his gaze and the way it broke through all the barriers she tried build between them.

Her orgasm crashed over her, and she couldn't think, couldn't speak, couldn't do anything but grip his shoulders harder and ride it out. It seemed to go on forever, her body pulsing around him. Just as she started to come down, he began thrusting harder, driving into her warmth over and over, seeking his own climax.

"Astrid." His voice sounded taut, desperate. "I'm going… I'm… I don't want to…"

She understood and managed to climb off right before he came. He erupted into his fist with a groan, eyes finally closing as his release overwhelmed him. Watching him, her heart tightened. Emotions welled inside her with an echo of Cecily's words. *Does he know that you're falling in love with him?*

Neither of them moved right away. The silence stretched out between them, first seconds, then minutes, like neither of them wanted to break it. Eli cleaned himself up with his undershirt, and Astrid shifted on the sofa, her muscles languid. She had no idea what would happen now. Eli ran a hand through his hair. After a pause, he reached over and ran a hand through her hair too, lightly stroking the top of her head. She stiffened in surprise before relaxing into his touch. He slid an arm around her shoulders and drew her against him. This was intimate, warm and sweet and tender in a way she hadn't expected. Affectionate.

Maybe her words were going to ruin the moment, but she had to know. "Are you going to tell me we shouldn't have done this?"

He shook his head. "I would think that's an exercise in futility at this point."

"Is it because you want me to finger your arse again?"

"Hush," he scolded. His sudden blush made her laugh, his

embarrassment visible all the way to the tips of his ears and down his neck.

Grinning, she leaned up. "I thought you'd like that, but I didn't realize how much you'd like it."

Eli looked away. "Let's not talk about it, all right?"

"What, you're shy now? Mr. Eli Rutledge is shy?" She ran a finger over his collarbone.

He pulled back an inch. "You know I'm shy."

"You're not shy."

He stared up at the ceiling, his expression thoughtful. "I'm not like you, though. I'm not like this." He gestured between them. "You just go after what you want, and the devil take whatever stands in your way." He looked back to her. "That's not me."

Astrid shifted in his arms. How strange to hear him talk of himself in that way, when he was a man people respected as a businessman and professional.

"You're right, you know," he added.

She reached up to play with the hair at the nape of his neck. "About my finger in your arse?"

"No. About what you said before." His expression shifted to resignation. "I don't want to share."

To avoid looking into his eyes, she studied his chest instead, tracing a pattern in the dark hair with her fingers. "I told you before, we're not in a relationship, so you don't get a say in this."

"A relationship is out of the question."

"Of course it is." At least her voice sounded more certain than she felt. This conversation would probably be a lot easier to have if his hand wasn't stroking up and down her back, caressing her skin like she was his lover and not just a casual fuck. He obviously liked her, but he completely resisted the idea of a relationship. His status must be so important that it superseded any feelings he might have. He wasn't the first man she'd had sex with, but he was the first who treated her like more than an enjoyable pastime. In moments like this, in the moments where they spoke like equals, he treated her like…like he could love her, maybe, someday.

But however he felt, he apparently wasn't going to move forward on those feelings.

"Let's make a deal, shall we?" he said.

Astrid hadn't expected that, and she looked up. Eli was watching her, a smile playing about his lips. "You do whatever you're going to do anyway, but you don't tell me about it. And in the meantime, we stop fighting whatever this is between us. Do we have a deal?"

It wasn't perfect. No emotions, no entanglements, no relationship, but it was better than nothing at all. Astrid smiled, and if her smile didn't reach her eyes, Eli didn't comment. "Deal."

The London Business Council did not suffer fools gladly, and their meeting room seemed designed to convey that impression as clearly as possible. As Eli took his seat at the long, mahogany table, he scanned the dull, beige wallpaper, the undecorated walls, the wooden mantel clock that was the room's only concession to decor. They had been meeting in that same room for over five years. Had it always been so drab?

Having arrived a few minutes early, he was able to watch the other members of the LBC arrive. He'd never noticed how sour they all looked: stern, lacking frivolity, unhappy in a way that seemed fashionable for men of his class. It gave them all a similar look, despite their physical differences in height, weight, and skin color. Even Leandor Hollbrook, the council member closest to his own age and a casual friend for several years, wore a grave expression as he settled down at the table next to Eli. Had something terrible happened and he was the only person unaware?

The evening began as normal, though, with its tedious

review of the minutes from their last meeting, so there was no unusual bad news. This was just everyone's mood. Maybe they were always this unpleasant, and he was finally noticing it.

"That brings us to the update on the World's Fair." The council chairman, Gowen Woodbridge, tapped his stack of papers to make them even. "The builders began construction last week, and the IFCT has scheduled their Judges' Viewing for next week on May twenty-seventh. I assume everyone is participating in the Fair?"

Around him, men nodded solemnly, a few also murmuring assent. Woodbridge scratched his graying beard. "After some negotiations, the IFCT has agreed to give members of the London Business Council prime placement in the fairgrounds. As pillars of the business community, your participation is essential to the continued high standards of the World's Fair. We cannot let the Fair descend into a rabble of disreputable merchants and swindlers as it has in other countries."

Around him, men nodded again, and Eli started to do the same out of habit. Then Astrid came to mind. He knew where she would fall on Woodbridge's continuum, the one with "pillars of the business community" on one end and "rabble of disreputable merchants and swindlers" on the other.

As if to confirm his assumptions, Woodbridge continued speaking. "We've enforced the mandate that all Fair participants must either be reputable businesses or sponsored by reputable businesses. Weed out the riffraff."

Eli held up a finger to catch Woodbridge's attention. The man stopped, eyebrows raised. "Yes, Mr. Rutledge?"

In all his time on the council, Eli rarely weighed in on the issues personally, but it felt imperative he speak up here.

"Aren't you worried that mandate excludes smaller businesses? Those without shopfronts, for example."

Woodbridge blinked a few times at him, eyebrows raised. "Yes, that's the general idea." After giving Eli another confused look, he continued speaking about the Fair and their responsibilities as a liaison organization to the IFCT. Eli tuned him out, though, and sank into his own thoughts.

He liked Gowen Woodbridge. The man had been a mentor to him when he had first taken his father's seat on the LBC, had guided him through the turbulent first years after the Revolution. He led the council fairly and with an eye on the future. Yet now, Eli couldn't help remembering the times that Gowen persuaded them to vote against expanding membership, emphasizing how a small core of committed businessmen was better than a large, nebulous organization. It had seemed like the best idea at the time, but countless small businesses had probably lost the opportunity to join the council as a result of that decision, and he'd never considered those ramifications. In fact, no new businesses had joined in the time Eli had been present. He'd taken his father's seat on the council nearly ten years earlier, and in those ten years, the membership had remained exactly the same.

When the meeting adjourned, Eli's colleague Leandor pulled him aside, eyebrows knitted in concern. That expression seemed at odds with his tousled blond curls and youthful face, the pale skin smooth and unlined. "What's gotten into you, mate? You were staring off into space for the whole last half of the meeting. Does this have anything to do with your top-secret World's Fair invention?" He smiled, but his smile was still tentative and hinted at larger worries.

"Actually, yes. I have a lot on my mind lately." Eli hesitated, not sure how much to tell Leandor. They weren't that close, but he wanted to confide in someone.

Leandor sized up his expression. "Why don't we go grab a pint?"

A half hour later, they were sitting in the Brass Whistle, a pub mostly frequented by other businessmen. Eli stared down into his drink while Leandor shifted on the next stool. "Are you going to tell me what this is all about, or what?" Leandor asked. "You were moping through the whole council meeting. I know the meetings are boring, but it was no different than usual."

Eli took a gulp of the strong, hoppy beer and set it down on the counter. "Leandor, do you know any women business owners here in London?"

Leandor rubbed his smooth-shaven chin, puzzling, before his face broke in a smile. "You mean like a brothel?"

"No, not like a brothel. I mean other than that."

"I don't know, let me think." Leandor drank from his own pint while he did so, staring up at the brass piping that ran its way around the ceiling. "The bird I bring my sewing to, she's a woman."

"And that's it? No others?"

"Not that I can think of. Women aren't really into business."

A month ago, he probably would have said the same thing. He stared down into his drink, the light-brown froth on his beer clinging wetly to the glass. "I don't think that's it, Leandor. I think it's our fault. The council for sure, maybe men in general. I think we keep women from getting a foothold in business."

"Is this about the World's Fair?" Leandor's brow furrowed.

This conversation wasn't fair to him, really. He had no idea what was behind Eli's comments.

Eli set his beer back down on the bar and rubbed his hands across the tops of his thighs, preparing himself for this explanation. "You know I'm entering the Fair," Eli began, and Leandor nodded. "I'm not doing it alone, though. I've partnered up with Astrid Bailey. She's a business owner, but she wasn't allowed to enter the Fair because she doesn't have a storefront. Not a 'reputable business,' they told her, without even knowing what she was selling."

"Why doesn't she open up a storefront?"

"Money, mostly, I'm sure. She hasn't come right out and said it, but that's got to be why." He took another swig of beer, leaning forward on the bar. Before meeting Astrid, he'd never considered his own privilege; he'd mostly thought about his difficult upbringing and how much he'd worked for his status.

Leandor rubbed his chin again. "Why are you partnering up with her? Why not enter on your own? You're going to have to split the prize money if you even win anything. Oh, is she giving you a bit o' skirt? Is that what this is all about?"

Eli gave him a scathing look. They shouldn't be talking about this. "Forget it."

"Sorry. I was only cocking about. Didn't mean to strike a nerve." Leandor looked into his own beer, temporarily subdued. After a moment, he looked back up at his friend. "Wait, are you in love with her?"

"Of course not." Eli set his beer down with such force that it sloshed up on the sides of the glass. "I don't have time for any of that frivolity."

Leandor shook his head. "Everybody needs somebody. You

can't go your whole life as a bachelor. Who'd take over the business, for one?"

Eli was beginning to regret this conversation. "It can't be Astrid." Maybe he could marry someone quiet, someone who'd find him suitable, but he couldn't get tangled up with a firecracker like her. That sort of relationship had a shelf life, and it was just until she found someone better. Maybe she'd already found that person in Cecily. Eli's stomach gave an unpleasant lurch.

"She's probably beneath you." Leandor nodded shrewdly. "Can't get mixed up in that. You're an influential man in this town, but you can kiss the LBC goodbye if you go shacking up with some working-class doll in a short skirt."

Eli winced. He knew men who refused to date outside of their social class, but he'd never given much thought to that aspect of his dynamic with Astrid. They were both business owners; certainly, he had more money than she did, but she was worldlier, wise in ways he'd never had to be. That basically made them equals. Before he could respond, Leandor continued. "Listen, mate, you don't owe this girl anything. You're doing her a favor by sponsoring her. Don't let her manipulate you into anything else, like buying her a shop or paying her bills."

Eli tried to keep his anger in check. "Astrid hasn't asked for any of that. She wouldn't ask for anything like that. She's not that kind of person."

"Well, then, if you're not in love with her and she's not asking you for anything, sounds like there's not a problem at all." He patted Eli on the back. "You're doing enough. The World's Fair, that's top-notch. You should feel good about that. Not everyone needs to be a council member, Eli. It's like

Gowen said. We can't let just anyone in, or the whole organization is meaningless."

Eli stared down into his beer again, not sure how to respond. Leandor didn't understand at all. Was Eli really jeopardizing his reputation by partnering with Astrid? Not in any substantial way, surely. The LBC was old-fashioned, yes, but they followed the law. He'd done his own research to confirm that felicitation devices were indeed perfectly legal, and they were a lark, a novelty that earned titters but ultimately did no harm. Besides, he'd been a member of the LBC for a decade, and his reputation was solid. Surely, he would be fine. Right?

Leandor moved on to another topic of conversation, but Eli had trouble listening.

22

Cecily seemed to understand that something had changed, even though Astrid hadn't told her anything yet. From the moment Cecily walked into the flat that Saturday morning, she watched Astrid with curious intensity. Astrid was happy to divert her attention onto the new products, which Cecily praised effusively.

"These are wonderful. Exactly what I was looking for." Cecily flicked the switches on each device in turn, first the smaller one then the larger one with the curve. Astrid beamed as Cecily marveled aloud about the attention to detail. Shaping the brass had taken a long time, hours spent over the flame, molding the casing and polishing it by hand. Her friendship with Cecily aside, it was nice to hear positive words about her efforts.

After setting the inventions aside, Cecily pulled Astrid into a hug. "You've done a lovely job. Thank you for all your hard work this week." She drew back and held Astrid at arm's length. "Now, what's happened between you and Eli?"

Astrid extricated herself from Cecily's grip, not sure how

to explain what had changed, if anything. "There was an incident." What a strange way to describe their intense sex on the workroom sofa. "I'm not sure what to think. I don't really want to talk about it."

Cecily patted her arm with a gentle hand. "You know, dear, I'm here for you if you need anything. All right?"

"All right." Relieved not to have to discuss him further, Astrid settled into the sofa. "I'm glad you like the devices."

Cecily responded immediately to the change of subject. "Yes, they're perfect. And that's something I'd like to talk with you about." She sat down next to Astrid. "Would you be interested in a permanent contract position with the Lahey Emporium?"

Astrid's heart skipped, and she leaned forward. "What would that look like?"

"You would be making felicitation devices. These and others. I could pay you a hundred pounds per month, plus all cost for materials."

Adrenaline rushed through Astrid in a swift current. "A hundred pounds?" That was enough to pay her rent, plus many of her expenses. She barely made that from her existing contracts. "Cecily, that's brilliant. I don't know what to say."

"So you'll accept? Say you'll accept." Cecily took both Astrid's hands in hers, her eyes bright.

"Of course I'll accept." She welcomed Cecily's hug, both light and dizzy at once. A hundred pounds for one contract? Suddenly her financial concerns didn't seem so bad.

When Cecily drew back, her face was alight. She seemed every bit as happy with the arrangement as Astrid. "Then maybe you don't need the World's Fair project anymore."

Astrid's smile faded. She opened her mouth to protest but

then closed it again, not sure exactly what to say. Cecily was right. The World's Fair project with Eli was a desperate attempt to make money, money she technically no longer needed.

But what about Eli? They had a partnership. Except...he already had a business. He didn't really need the World's Fair, either. If they ended things now, they could both walk away with no further entanglements.

So why was she so reluctant to accept Cecily's offer?

Reading Astrid's facial expression, Cecily patted her arm. "It's all right. Only a suggestion. The World's Fair will be over next month anyway, right?"

"Right." Astrid sighed. "I guess none of this will matter in a few weeks."

"Can you do one initial order at least, if you're not sure about the contract? I'll want one of everything for starters and then ten more of each of these." Cecily gestured to the new designs resting on the table. "How long will that take?"

"One of everything?" Astrid tucked a loose strand of hair behind her ear and looked over at the dozen or so items in her display case. These were all familiar builds to her, so it wouldn't take very long. "I imagine I can have a full set of the older models for you inside of about two weeks. The new ones will take longer, unless I can cast some molds. I imagine about a month, maybe three weeks, after I finish the first order."

"That seems fine." From her purse, Cecily produced a stack of ten-pound notes and counted them out into Astrid's hand. Each crisp bill made Astrid's heart beat faster. "You can invoice me for materials costs at the end of each month. One of everything first, and we'll hold off on anything more perma-nent for now. All right?"

"All right."

Cecily put her money away, and then silence stretched between them. Finally, she asked, "Do you want me to stay?"

Astrid looked at her lovely face, her kind eyes, her warm smile. This woman was her closest friend at the moment. With a word, she could have Cecily in her arms again, in her bed, making love to her with lips and tongue until neither of them could think. It was tempting, but something had changed inside her, and she didn't want to be distracted tonight. She had a lot of thinking to do.

"I'd like to be alone. It's...not you."

Cecily smiled. "I thought you might say that." She kissed Astrid then stood. "When can I see you again?"

Astrid got up as well to show her out. "Maybe next week? I need some time to think."

"Of course. Just drop me a line." With a swirl of skirts, she was gone.

After she left, Astrid leaned her back against the door and closed her eyes.

A noise from the back of the flat made her open them. A glass canister rested in the delivery tube. Astrid opened it up to see another letter from Josian. In the three weeks she'd been gone, Josian had written every few days. Each reply Astrid had sent was perfunctory, friendly without being intimate, leaving out most of the details of her life. She'd confessed to partnering up with Eli for the World's Fair, but she didn't share the nature of their relationship, nor any information about Cecily. It had all happened so quickly; she could hardly believe this was her life now. How was she supposed to describe it to Josian when she couldn't make sense of it herself?

Different paths stretched out in front of her. Without worrying much about how she was going to pay her bills next month, she was faced with the far more difficult question she'd been avoiding all along. What did she really want?

Turning her back on the question, she went to read Josian's letter.

23

———————

When Eli arrived at the workshop Sunday morning, he wasn't surprised to be the first one there. He had taken to arriving earlier and earlier each time they worked, wanting more time without Astrid's distracting presence. They were almost finished crafting the Ossy, and he couldn't afford to keep getting sidetracked. After lighting the lamps, he settled right in to assemble the gear housing.

Morning stretched on, though, and Astrid didn't arrive. He didn't notice at first, focused entirely on his work. When he took a break for a drink, he realized he was still alone in the shop. A quick check of his pocket watch revealed that she was more than two hours late. Immediately he imagined a dozen terrible circumstances. He should go look for her.

As if she knew he was beginning to worry, she appeared in the doorway then, breathless. "'Lo. I'm sorry I'm late."

Eli wiped sweat from his brow with a rolled-up shirtsleeve. He couldn't identify the emotion in her eyes. "What's wrong, Astrid?"

She bit her lip. "I've been thinking. Maybe we should give up on this."

"What?" Eli put down his spanner. "You're kidding, right? We've been working on this for weeks. The Judges' Viewing is less than a week away. You can't give up now."

Walking into the workroom, she looked around as if seeing it all for the first time. She pushed herself onto the worktable with her legs dangling. "Cecily offered me a permanent contract position making products for the Lahey Emporium. I'm thinking I'm going to take it."

Eli scratched his beard. "I don't understand. She said you had to stop working on this? Was that a condition of the offer?"

"No, it's just that… Well, I don't need the money anymore, and we've been having such a difficult time with each other lately. If we gave up now, I could save you the hassle of putting up with me." Her smile didn't reach her eyes.

None of this made sense. This was Astrid's dream, winning the World's Fair, opening her shop. "How much is she paying you? If you don't mind me asking."

"A hundred pounds a month." She spread her hands, palm up, and gave a small shrug. "It's enough to pay my bills and a little extra, plus she's covering material costs."

"That's not enough to open your shop, though. You'd need World's Fair winnings to do that." She was giving up, right in front of him.

"Maybe I don't really need a shop. Maybe I can just keep working from my house. This—you and me—this is all ridiculous, right? It's a pipe dream. The Ossy can't win the World's Fair." She put her hand on the saddle, expression wistful.

Watching her lose faith like this stirred something inside

him. He sat on the bench in front of her, looking up into her eyes. "Astrid, please don't give up. We're almost finished. Let's see this through." He took her hands, so delicate in his much larger ones, delicate but strong. "If this is about last week, I'm sorry. I can stay away from you if it helps. But the World's Fair is important to you. To...me. To us. Will you stick with it, for me? I think we have a chance."

She met his gaze, unexpected vulnerability filling her eyes. She always seemed so strong, and her weakness brought forth tenderness in him that he didn't fully understand. If she were like this all the time, vulnerable and willing to confide in him, he could fall in love with her. He could risk it. Maybe. Maybe, if she loved him back, he could open himself up to that kind of chance. The thought made him dizzy, and he couldn't deal with it right then.

At last, she nodded. "All right. I suppose we can keep going." With a deep breath, she pushed herself to her feet and began rolling up the sleeves on her blouse. "What's next, then?"

For the next few hours, they completed the final steps of assembling the Ossy. Working together had never seemed so effortless; they built in perfect complement to each other, motions nearly in sync, their mutual goal uniting them. He wondered what it would be like to work with her like this all the time. She built with the same methodical precision he prized, with an attention to detail that was second to none. She fastened each component with precise tensioning, bent over the control panel, her hair occasionally falling across her brow. Once, she caught him staring, and her cheeky smile sent him back to work feeling disarmed.

Hours later, Eli soldered the final connection in place,

attaching the control panel while Astrid screwed the shaft into its housing. They finished at about the same time, looked at each other, then back at the machine.

"I think that's it, then." Eli stepped back to admire their creation.

The Ossy was beautiful. Brass piping supported the entire structure. The saddle was covered with sleek red leather and all the attachments were in place. The machine gleamed in the lamplight, shining and polished and ready to be displayed at the World's Fair. He knew he was beaming, and Astrid's face glowed with pride as well.

"It's lovely." She ran her hand across the saddle, touched the brass rivets holding the leather in place, then grasped the shaft in a decidedly inappropriate way. With each twist of a dial, she tested the components, and when everything had passed muster, she turned to Eli and wrapped her arms around him, the unexpected hug taking his breath away. "Thank you. I can't believe it's finished."

He held her close against him, some emotion blocking his throat. Pride? Exhaustion? Tenderness? Something more. Whatever it was, she didn't seem to notice and soon pulled away to begin talking through plans for transporting the Ossy to the Judges' Viewing the following weekend. Although she'd stepped away, his chest was still warm from the press of her body, and he had to fight to drag his attention back to the present conversation.

Falling in love with Astrid was a terrible idea. He needed to find a way to stop it from happening.

24

———

The day dawned brightly, an auspicious omen if Astrid were the sort to believe in omens. With the sun shining on the back of her neck, she waited outside the train station for Eli to arrive with the Ossy. Feeling a bit self-conscious, she looked down at her traditional attire, her bustled skirt and short-waisted jacket over a high-collared blouse. He might not even recognize her.

The crowd parted to reveal a giant wooden crate on a motorized dolly making its way across the street toward her, a pair of feet barely visible behind it. Eli peered around the crate with a grin as he pulled up alongside her. The flutter in her chest was undoubtedly nerves about the Judges' Viewing, and not because she hadn't seen him in a week and had missed him. She was going to stick to that story.

He looked her up and down. "Look at you! You're like a proper woman."

"Very nice, you bastard." She punched his arm affectionately, but inside, she was a bundle of nerves. "Are you ready for this?"

"Of course I'm ready. We're going to be brilliant." He flashed her another smile.

Hard to tell if he really believed that or was just trying to reassure her. Then the train roared into the station with a great screech of brakes and a billow of steam, and any comments she would have made were drowned in the sudden commotion. Eli began guiding the dolly forward onto the train, and she could do nothing but follow behind him, apprehension blossoming inside her.

The Judges' Viewing was being held at the fairgrounds, which she had yet to see. Outside the windows, the town whizzed past her, a blur of skyscrapers and tenements and distant skyline, and Eli's leg pressed against hers with comforting warmth. They had squeezed the Ossy's crate into the storage space behind them, and it loomed at the edges of her peripheral vision, a reminder of their purpose.

After a few minutes of silence, during which they both stared out the window, Astrid broached the thought that had been on her mind all day. "I think you should be ready for what we might face in there."

Eli dismissed her comment with a hand wave. "This is my third World's Fair. It's the Judges' Viewing. We'll have a closed booth, like all the other participants, and the judges will come in as a group. They'll ask us some questions and mark things down, and then they'll leave. When they finish, they'll tell me where my booth will be for the Fair." He shrugged. "It's all routine."

Of course that would have been his experience exhibiting his work to others. She seldom faced the same "routine" treatment. "The Fair judges are old-fashioned. I don't know how they're going to feel about the Ossy."

"Oh, is that what you're worried about?" He patted her hand. "Astrid, I'm a member of the London Business Council. I have some influence in this community. I have a good reputation, and I'm sure that will be enough to overcome any reluctance on the judges' part."

He seemed so sure; she didn't want to try to dissuade him. As the train roared on to their destination, though, she remained full of doubt.

The site of the fairgrounds was a ten-acre plot of land on the outskirts of Yorkdam, at the edge of the West Chester moors, one of the only places where so much open land could still be found in Brittania. Astrid rarely traveled this far from home, and when she stepped off the train car, the scent of the air was so different that she just stood, breathing, while Eli unloaded the Ossy. Shaking herself back to awareness, she helped him fire up the dolly's engine. When they stepped out from behind the train station, she glimpsed the fairgrounds for the first time.

As far as she could see, booths and brightly colored banners stretched out across what had previously been open countryside. Giant flags of red and blue snapped in the wind. Over the arched entrance, an immense banner announced the Fair. As she and Eli pushed the Ossy through that arch, Astrid tried to look everywhere at once, unable to absorb the sights fast enough. Steam engines whirred right inside the main gates, sending power through giant looping cables running out and along the paths, which were lined with wooden booths waiting for the businesses that had rented them. Two men were inflating a large balloon that could be a zeppelin or a dirigible, their muscles straining against shirtsleeves as they turned cranks and hauled the support ropes into place. Many men were swinging sledgehammers, driving tent pegs into the earth, raising canvas monstrosities for central exhibits in between the booths. Everywhere, young boys were running at full sprint between work stations, carrying armfuls of pipes, stakes, rope, or fabric. And on all sides, accompanying Astrid and Eli down the main path, were hundreds of other hopeful inventors pushing large crates or toting bundles wrapped in cloth.

The throng moved as one toward the administrative offices, hub of the Judges' Viewing area. A full-bearded official, who seemed mostly occupied by shouting instructions to the crowd at large, finally took a break from shouting to find their name on a master roster and thrust a ticket into Eli's hand. Astrid was dizzy from the commotion as they were ushered down a narrow path to one of hundreds of tiny booths closed off with canvas hangings. Eli lifted the heavy front flap and pushed the Ossy inside.

The small booth was warm and smelled like hay. Astrid flicked a switch to the one lamp hanging in the corner, flooding the space with yellow light.

Eli read from the ticket they'd been given. "Shit."

"What?"

He tapped the ticket. "So much for my council position getting us an advantage. We're not scheduled for our viewing for another hour and a half."

Astrid took the ticket to read the time then set it aside on top of the crate. "It could be worse. Some people will probably be here all day. Let's get unpacked."

Together, they unfastened the walls of their packing crate and began setting up the Ossy. It conveniently broke down into three parts, and assembly took fifteen minutes of their hour-and-a-half wait. Afterward, they had nothing to do but sit and be thankful that the Fair Committee had at least given them chairs.

In the dim, small interior of the booth, Eli seemed to take up more than his share of space. Perhaps it was the fact that the Ossy took up half the room, but he still was so close, she could smell his cologne, which reminded her of the smell of his bare skin.

This was not a path she should continue down. The room was already too warm, and thinking about Eli's body against hers was making her hotter. If she began fanning herself, would it be too obvious? She unfastened the buttons of her jacket and hung the offending article over the back of the chair, noticing Eli's eyes travel to her breasts pressing against the buttons of her blouse, their curves lifted by her underbust corset, When propriety dictated he should look away, he did not. His tongue barely brushed against his bottom lip as he studied her.

"Can I help you?"

Eli nodded without apology, his eyes finally moving up to meet hers. "You know, Astrid, I think we've made a misstep."

Unease washed over her. "What do you mean?"

Getting up, he touched the Ossy, his hand lingering on the saddle, where the shaft was hidden down out of sight. "We never tested the finished machine."

Astrid swallowed hard. He couldn't be suggesting what he was suggesting.

Reading the expression on her face, he smiled, mischief sparkling in his eyes. He tugged her to her feet, pulling her against him, one large hand sliding to the center of her back. "We're all alone, Astrid. Are you feeling wicked?"

She barely recognized this man. Just a few weeks ago, he had shied away from any contact with her. That Eli would never have suggested this incredibly lurid act in this very public place. Worse was how she wanted to give in, how her body thrummed with sudden arousal and the adrenaline of risk. "Eli, anyone could come in."

"But they won't. I've been here before. We'll be in here for an hour, at least. Plenty of time."

"They'll hear the machine."

"Of course they will. It's a World's Fair, machines are running everywhere." He dipped his head to nuzzle against her ear, his lips brushing the tender skin and sending a shiver down her spine. "What do you say?"

"I don't know," she murmured, the *yes* lingering just behind it. He kissed her, and thinking became exponentially more difficult. He tasted good, like rich coffee. The languid precision of his kiss made her legs go boneless and unsteady, and she clung to him to keep her balance, returning the kiss with her own intensity. When she gently bit his lower lip, he rewarded her with a low moan.

She bumped into the Ossy. During their kiss, he'd backed her up to the machine. Pulling back, he looked down at her with heavy-lidded eyes. "Say yes, Astrid. I want to watch you come."

He cupped both her breasts in his hands. She gasped, arousal rushing through her like fire. Even through the material of her blouse, his thumbs against her nipples teased them into taut peaks immediately. She was already getting wet. The machine pressed solidly against her back, a delectable temptation of immediate, overwhelming pleasure. And Eli would be watching her the whole time, like in her most wanton fantasies. A shiver ran down her spine.

"They'll know." Her protest sounded breathy and weak, and she was smiling now.

"No one will know." He smiled back, and it was obvious he knew he'd won. He kissed her lips again. "Or we can sit here for another hour and you can think about how good it would feel to come."

Fuck, the man knew how to take her apart.

Her hands trembled as she folded down the knee rests they'd installed on each side of the saddle. Padded and covered with red leather, they would hold her a few inches above the Ossy. Eli nudged a low latch with his foot, and two steps folded down with a rattle and fell into place, like on a stagecoach. Holding Eli's hand for support, she stepped up and knelt over the saddle, settling into place. The leather was cool against her overheated cleft.

"No underthings again? Even today?"

Astrid flashed him a cheeky smile. "Never."

The control panel in front of her displayed a series of knobs and dials to control the various components of the Ossy. She licked her lips, adjusting the settings to her preference. Her skirts fell over the tops of her thighs, hiding the most intimate details from Eli, who was looking at her as if he wanted to devour her whole. He stepped up to the front of the Ossy, his body mere inches from hers, and kissed her again.

With a start, the knee pads dropped several inches. She cried out into Eli's mouth as she landed harder onto the saddle, the knee pads suddenly a few inches lower than they had been. Eli smiled wickedly, his eyes alight, as she caught her breath. "Can't have you getting away, can we?"

Astrid shifted. This position left her helpless to lift off the Ossy without assistance, and she knew how the machine would pull her climax mercilessly from her body. Eli was waiting, hands near the controls, for her to give him the okay.

She nodded, and he flipped the switches all at once.

A strangled sound slipped from her mouth as the ridge beneath her clit began vibrating, the intensity rendering her speechless. She had to be quiet. Astrid pressed her lips together as the shaft pressed upward, parting her folds, penetrating her with ruthless inexorability. This cock was slightly larger than the last, and it stretched her, delving deeper and deeper. Oh, God, maybe she had set it too high and it was going to split her open, but it reversed just at the moment she was completely filled. She let her hands fall away as the shaft withdrew, moving at the same torturously slow pace. Her hands fluttered down to her thighs, digging into the material of her skirt, needing to hold on to something.

"Faster?" Eli's voice was a low rumble in her ears.

She nodded, eyes still closed. The dial clicked, and the shaft speed doubled. She held back a whimper.

"Open your eyes, Astrid. I want you to see me watching you."

Eli stood in front of her, his eyes dark and hooded, studying her as she was relentlessly fucked by the machine. His eyes never leaving hers, he turned the intensity of the vibrator higher on the dial. She stifled a needy sound, reflexively trying to move away but unable to do so. Already the crescendo of arousal was building, building, faster than it ever had before. It was too intense, and she tried again to shift back away from the vibrations, but that only served to seat her more firmly on the shaft, which was filling her over and over again. There was no way to escape the pleasure threatening to overtake her.

"That's right. Give in to it." Eli unfastened his trousers and freed his cock, already fully erect. She couldn't take her eyes away as he wrapped his hand around it and began to stroke. "Do you like to watch me too?"

The sight left her breathless. She nodded.

A sudden spasm wrung a moan out of her, and she clapped her hand over her mouth. Eli smiled, continuing to stroke himself. "Quiet, now. Don't want anyone else to hear you. Can you do that? Can you come without making a sound?"

His low, husky voice made her shiver. Her pussy clenched involuntarily around the shaft, its firm, unyielding surface still thrusting into her. She could barely think, could focus on nothing but the sight of Eli stroking himself and the intensity building between her legs. She gripped her breasts, cupping them, squeezing the nipples, desperate for the extra stimulation. Eli groaned low.

"Fuck, Astrid, you're going to kill me." He sank into a chair, his hand moving faster over his erection, still watching her like he was unable to look away.

Astrid was reaching the point of no return, a brutally swift climb toward orgasm. Tight spirals of sensation coiled low inside her. She pressed her lips together, willing herself not to cry out as the vibrator teased her clit and the shaft plunged into her again and again. In the last moments before she came, she locked eyes with Eli, who was watching her agape as his hand worked furiously over his cock.

Climax crashed through her with such intensity that she thought she might pass out, and she held her breath through it, trying not to make a noise as she rocked between pleasure and overwhelm. The Ossy was merciless, the vibrator continuing to buzz away against her overly sensitive clit, the shaft still thrusting at its punishing pace. Before she could even reach for the controls, she was peaking again.

Eli gave a soft groan in front of her, and she managed to catch sight of him just as he threw his head back, hips thrusting upward into thin air as he reached his pinnacle. As she watched him ride out his release, her second climax came headlong on the heels of her first, making the world dissolve around her.

Coming back to herself, panting from lack of oxygen, she swatted at the controls and brought the machine to a stop. She collapsed forward, still throbbing between her legs. After a moment, Eli was there beside her, somehow already composed, lifting her off the machine as if she were weightless. He set her down gingerly in his chair and began cleaning the Ossy.

That task complete, Eli sat down on the chair next to her and pulled her into his lap. She relaxed into him, enjoying his warm body against hers, deliciously sated and surprisingly unembarrassed by the whole situation.

Eli's rumbling laugh startled her. "What?" she asked.

"Only about forty-five minutes left to wait."

25

Disoriented, Astrid took a moment to realize she'd fallen asleep on Eli's chest, and she'd woken because he'd said something. "Hmm?" She blinked.

"I said it's almost time. They'll be here soon. Come on."

She straightened up, rubbing sleep away from her eyes. She could still smell Eli on her skin, a souvenir from napping in his arms, and the scent lingered as she adjusted her appearance to some form of respectability. When her hair was straightened and her jacket buttoned, she inspected the Ossy itself. Eli had cleaned it to sparkling perfection, all signs of their impropriety removed. A few hand-cranks lowered the shaft to the down position, and to the uninformed, the device resembled nothing more than a particularly sumptuous saddle.

"Here, take a look at the paperwork. See if there's anything you want me to change." Eli held out a sheaf of papers for her to leaf through. At the top of the first page was the name and specifications of their machine in Eli's fine, neat handwriting.

For his description of the machine's function, he had chosen his words carefully, with a finesse for language and euphemism she definitely lacked.

"It passes inspection?" He fastened the buttons on his suit coat, watching her skim over the documentation.

She could spot nothing wrong. "It does." Her smile felt tight on her face, anxiety resurfacing with their imminent judging.

The hubbub outside their booth grew louder, and Astrid couldn't resist lifting the door hanging to peek outside. The bright sunlight assaulted her eyes after the dimness of the booth, and she had to squint and blink to see anything at all.

When she ducked her head back inside, it took a moment for her eyes to adjust again. "They're right next door. I saw a group of men going into this booth right here." She gestured to the hangings next to them, where the dull murmur of voices barely penetrated the din outside. The moments seemed to stretch on endlessly before at last their own tent hangings were lifted, and four men stepped into their tiny booth.

Between their somber expressions and their dark clothes, they could have all been pressed from the same mold. The only difference was in ages; one man's whiskers had gone gray, while two others were salt-and-pepper, and the youngest had almost no gray at all. Beyond that, it was hard to tell them apart—similar average heights, similar average builds, similar intense focus on their paperwork.

At last one of the salt-and-pepper men adjusted his small, round glasses and looked up at them. "Ah, Mr. Rutledge. It's good to see you again." He extended his hand to Eli with a smile.

"Good to see you, Mr. Pilbright." Eli shook the man's hand. "Miss Bailey, Mr. William Pilbright. He and I are acquainted from the International Federation for Commerce and Trade."

Mr. Pilbright shook Astrid's hand. This led to other introductions to each of the other judges, whom Eli did not already know. Finally, when hands had been shaken and tight smiles exchanged, they turned their attention to the Bailey-Rutledge Oscillating Felicitator.

Pilbright led the investigation, whether because he knew Eli or because he was in charge, Astrid wasn't sure. First they pored over Eli's documentation, identical furrowed eyebrows on their faces. Then, they examined the machine itself, walking around it, expressions stern, albeit a bit confused. Graybeard Man—she'd already forgotten everyone's names but Pilbright—peered into the saddle where the shaft was nearly out of sight, then he turned to the other three men and called them closer. No one turned on the machine or went anywhere near the controls. They murmured to each other in a huddle, and even though Astrid tried to eavesdrop, she couldn't hear much over the noises outside their booth.

Finally, they broke apart, and the scowls on their faces were not encouraging. Astrid's stomach twinged again with anxiety. Pilbright addressed Eli directly, as if Astrid weren't even in the room.

"Is there some kind of joke here, Rutledge?" Pilbright looked down at the papers then back up at Eli.

Eli frowned. "I don't understand. What do you mean? This is our invention for the World's Fair contest."

Next to Pilbright, the other Salt-And-Pepper Man scowled more deeply. "Do you mean to tell me that you expect this machine to be on display, in front of the God-fearing people of London? Spreading your message of depravity?"

She should probably let Eli do the talking, but his frozen, wide-eyed stare made her step forward. "There's nothing depraved about any of this. Self-pleasure is a perfectly normal and natural act. I sell felicitation devices to women of all backgrounds in accordance with the laws of London, and this is merely another device of the same ilk."

"We haven't treated hysteria as a disease in decades." Graybeard's face was turning a reddish-purple color from the neck up, but he was at last addressing her directly. "What you're proposing has no medical purpose whatsoever. It replaces the marriage bed with some sort of mechanical filth."

"Excuse me, gentlemen." Eli had found his voice. "You're being unreasonable. This is a product to meet a need. As Miss Bailey said, there is no law against any sort of felicitation device, and it would serve the lonely women of our community and provide a marital aid to those who struggle with the physicality of their nuptials."

Salt-and-Pepper Man shook his head. "There may not be a law against this sort of thing, but that doesn't mean it's welcome in the World's Fair contest. There's a difference between *legal* and *moral*. We are a dignified affair. And you, a member of the London Business Council? You of all people should know better."

Before Astrid could say anything, Pilbright began speaking again. "Mr. Rutledge, I'm surprised you would put your name behind something like this. You are an upstanding member of the community with a very successful business. This type of investment could ruin you." He stepped closer to Eli, giving a sidelong glance at the Ossy, and his tone became more urgent.

"Do you think the LBC wants their name tied in with this sort of claptrap? I don't know what game you think you're playing here, but if you don't choose your associates carefully, you'll find yourself out of the council faster than you can imagine." When Pilbright looked at Astrid, his eyes were flinty, any previous kindness gone. It was obvious what kind of associates he opposed.

Graybeard clapped Pilbright on the shoulder. "That's enough of this nonsense. Mr. Rutledge, we'll consider this a temporary lapse in judgment and expect to hear or see no more of it. I look forward to seeing what sorts of wholesome products you'll be exhibiting at the Fair next week. You're young, Mr. Rutledge, and a few business indiscretions are to be expected, but I hope you'll show more sense in the future."

Pilbright tore their documents in half and dropped them in the straw behind him, and the group left.

Astrid stood rooted to the spot, numb with shock, anger slowly swelling within her. How dare they say such things about her and Eli? Those stodgy old men wouldn't know pleasure if it bit them on the arse. She turned to Eli, expecting to see the same outrage on his face.

Instead, he was already packing up, head down, dismantling the Ossy and loading it into its packing crate.

"That's it?" She couldn't believe it. "You're done? He insults us, and you just pack up and go quietly? You don't even fight?"

Eli looked up, his eyes haunted. "What do you expect me to do, Astrid? Fight back against the judges? Tell them they're wrong? Jeopardize my entire business and my standing in the community?"

Of course. Her anger still rose inside her, only now it had a much closer target. "You're just worried about your precious reputation. Worried about associating with women like me, right? That I'm going to cost you your good name with my wild ways?" She knew her voice was getting louder, but she couldn't help it. Eli's passivity infuriated her. She couldn't seem to stop yelling in her disappointment and her pain. "I should have quit when I wanted to. Getting into a partnership was a stupid idea."

"Can't accept help from anybody, can you?" He slammed the front wall of the crate into place, the crack of wood on wood echoing even over the din. If he'd seemed ambivalent before, he was certainly angry now. "I cared about this too, Astrid. But now it's finished. You need to learn when to give up. Go take Cecily's contract. At least there's one person in the world you feel comfortable enough to trust."

Astrid bristled. Something huge and ugly rose up inside her, clouding her vision, making it difficult for her to speak. The small space seemed impossibly claustrophobic now, their dalliance on the Ossy a lifetime ago. "At least Cecily treats me like an equal. She isn't worried about sullying herself with me."

Shoulder muscles bunched in anger, Eli hammered the nails into place to seal the crate. Each swing of the hammer punctuated his words. "Right. I don't care about you at all. That's why I rented the flat, bought all the equipment, worked day and night for weeks to get this goddamned machine built."

"Oh, so that's all because you *care* about me? It has nothing at all to do with the fact that you didn't have an idea for the Fair?" She wiped her face, angry that she was crying, angry that he could make her cry. "Here's news for you, Mr.

Rutledge. When people care about each other, they don't stand by and let other people insult them. You didn't even defend me!"

Eli slammed the hammer down on the top of the crate. "What do you want from me, Astrid? You want me to give up my whole life? Quit the LBC, destroy my business? For what? For some ungrateful, overly independent woman who won't even tell me how she feels about me?"

For a long moment, they stared at each other, and the words hung between them like a physical wall. Tears burned hot against Astrid's cheeks. She knew what he was asking of her. How could she tell him she loved him? How could she risk her heart again when he so clearly put his reputation above her? He wanted too much.

But how could she remain silent, knowing he was about to walk away?

While she stood there, her throat tight, trying to decide what to say, Eli kicked the switch that fired up the engine on the dolly. "That's what I thought. I'll have this delivered to your flat next week."

He pushed past her, leaving Astrid standing in the dim, empty booth, her heartbeat echoing in the space he left behind.

26

Eli slammed down the spanner so hard onto his workbench that the cash register rang. He hadn't been able to get Astrid off his mind since leaving her at the Judges' Viewing Saturday. How dare she accuse him of not caring, after all he'd done for her? She *knew* how hard he'd worked for his reputation and to keep his business afloat, and she wanted him to throw it all away. Now, he faced another miserable Monday morning, no one in his shop, and another goddamned watch to assemble with no end in sight. Was this his future? A lonely lifetime bent over pocket watches?

It was even sunny. Somehow that made him feel worse. When it was raining, as it so frequently did in London, he was able to justify his glumness. With the sun shining, though, his own negativity was cast into sharp relief against the beauty of the spring day. He leaned on his worktable with a sigh, staring out the front windows. He had no idea what would become of him.

The World's Fair was opening the following weekend. That information felt more like a burden than a joy; his two previous Fairs had been immensely successful, bringing in substantial revenue and dozens of new mail-order customers, but he didn't even know if he wanted to exhibit anymore. Maybe he should say to hell with all of it, give up his booth, and let someone else deal with the mess. He wouldn't do that, of course—those sorts of thoughts were irresponsible. Eli Rutledge was nothing if not *responsible*. Even in his mind, the words sounded bitter.

Astrid hadn't been far from his mind since Saturday afternoon, and he thought of her again as he drummed his fingers on the worktable. Surely he had done the right thing. Logic and reason told him that yes, he had acted properly; they also reminded him that getting too close to her had been a bad idea from the beginning. At least he'd escaped with his reputation and business intact.

Logic and reason felt sour, though, and had grown ever more so since leaving her on Saturday. The hurt expression on her face, the angry tears she kept swiping away with the back of her hand, pained him anew each time he remembered. Apparently this was who he was now. He was a man who put his reputation above his feelings. Above what he knew in his heart was right.

The bell above the door chimed. Sunlight spilled across the hardwood floors as a lovely woman stepped over the threshold, a blue parasol perched over her shoulder. She didn't walk so much as sweep over to him. As she approached, he stepped around the counter to survey her. The woman was all curves and softness, her ample bosom accented by a tan corset against her deep-blue skirt and blouse. Her long red curls spilled down her back. Why did she seem so familiar? He had never met her in person, he was sure; he would have remembered someone so striking.

"So it's you, then." With no introduction, she looked him up and down, tapping her fingertips against her lips and shaking her head.

"I'm sorry? I don't believe we've met." He held out a hand. "Eli Rutledge."

"I know who you are." She let him take her hand and kiss it formally, one eyebrow arched. "I'm Cecily Lahey. I'm here to see if you're really worth all this fuss."

Eli straightened. So this was Astrid's lover, the woman he'd caught a glimpse of in the doorway. He had no idea what she meant by "worth all the fuss." He tried a smile. "Can I help you with anything?"

Cecily dropped her handbag down on the counter with a thud. "You've made a regular arse out of yourself, you know."

Eli's mouth dropped open. He'd never even met the woman, and she had the nerve to talk to him so rudely? Before he could even respond, she cut him off.

"Don't bother to deny it. Astrid told me everything, poor girl. You've destroyed her. Never thought I'd see that girl with a broken heart, tough as she is, but congratulations. You're the bloke who's done it."

"Wait a minute." He held up a hand. "Astrid and I had a business arrangement for the World's Fair. Nothing more."

"Oh, right, a business arrangement." Cecily leaned on the counter and shook her head. "Tell me, Mr. Rutledge, do you always fuck your business associates?"

A blush rose hot up his neck, his anger and embarrassment mingling. Even though he knew they were alone, he looked around his shop automatically to see if anyone had heard. He picked up the pocket watch he'd been fixing and began turning it over in his hand, needing something to fiddle with. "I'm sorry. I don't see how any of this is your business. Just because Astrid's slept with both of us doesn't mean you're privy to the details. And I don't know what you want from me, but—"

Cecily cut him off. "I want to know how you feel about Astrid Bailey."

The watch slipped out of his hand and clattered to the counter again. He snatched it up and closed his fingers around it, the edges pressing into his palm. "And why should I tell you that? Did she send you here?"

Cecily sighed. "Of course not. I'm here because I want Astrid to be happy, and she seems to think she'd be happy with you. Lord knows why, since apparently you can't get your head out of your arse. Is it true you wouldn't even defend her to the Fair judges?" Cecily rested her chin on her hand, her eye contact making Eli more uncomfortable with each passing minute. He looked back down at the watch.

"None of this is my fault. I can't change the fact that World's Fair judges are old-fashioned. We tried, we failed, and that's it." He tossed the watch back down onto the counter. "She was going to quit the build, anyway, when she took your contract. I don't think she even cares." He knew it was a lie even as he said it.

Cecily rolled her eyes. "Have you really been spending this much time with her, and you don't think she cares?"

Eli met Cecily's eyes again, guilt flooding through him. Of course Astrid cared. He'd seen the light in her eyes when she spoke about her shop, the way her face glowed with pride when he complimented her work. This mattered to her. The

Ossy mattered, the World's Fair mattered, and her shop mattered. She'd put her hopes in him, and he'd let her down.

"I didn't mean to hurt her."

"Of course you didn't. Men never do." Cecily straightened up. "So, do you want to help her?"

He laughed bitterly, spinning the watch around with his fingertip. "She won't accept my help, I'm sure."

"She doesn't want pity, Mr. Rutledge. But that doesn't mean she won't accept your help. Especially if you admit that you're in love with her."

Eli's mouth went dry.

Cecily smiled. "I can always tell these things. It goes with my business, you might say."

He found his voice. "This comes back to the same thing I said to Astrid. You're asking me to risk my reputation for a woman who won't even tell me how she feels about *me*."

Cecily looked skyward. "I swear, you and Astrid are two of the most stubborn people I've ever met. If you don't know how she feels without her saying it, then I don't think I can help you."

Eli rubbed his thumb across the watch face. "Women like Astrid don't fall in love with men like me."

"You mean stubborn, pretentious bastards?"

"I mean boring businessmen." Eli squeezed his fingers around the watch again. "I loved a woman once, a strong, independent woman like Astrid, and she never loved me back. I put myself out there, and it destroyed me. Do you know what that's like?" He looked to Cecily, feeling desperate, exposed, pouring his heart all over the counter in front of a complete stranger.

Cecily's eyes were tight, her mouth set, no longer teasing

him. "If you're going to lock yourself away here in your shop and grow old with your watch parts and your loneliness, then I'll leave. But if you aren't ready to give up on Astrid, then maybe I can help."

Eli spun the watch in his fingers over and over again. What if she was right? If he had a chance for a do-over, was it worth risking everything?

Cecily snatched the watch out of his fingers and set it back down on the counter out of reach. "Stop playing with that and listen to me. I have an idea for how you can win Astrid back. But if you can't open your heart, or if your business reputation will be forever ruined by association with felicitation devices, you should tell me to go, and you can resume your solitude."

Eli weighed the consequences. Surely, Cecily was going to suggest something that could sully his good name, some sort of action from which his business might never recover. He'd have to risk heartbreak. In return, he'd have Astrid, with all her courage and independence, and maybe a chance at happiness, a chance he thought he'd lost.

He came to a decision more quickly than he'd anticipated.

"I'm listening."

27

———

By the time the doorbell rang at seven o'clock on Thursday evening, Astrid had finished the first order of felicitation devices for Cecily, as well as half a bottle of wine. She'd also made what was perhaps the greatest misstep of her friendship with Josian by writing her the truth, the entire truth, all the bullshit she'd been dealing with for the past month. When she sobered up, she might regret sending that glass canister back up the delivery tube, but for now, the wine meant she felt very little at all. She opened the door with a less than steady hand.

Cecily gave her a hug as soon as she entered. Immediately, she pulled back. "Goodness, Astrid, have you been drinking?"

"Yep." Astrid made her way over to the sofa and sank down, putting her feet up on the coffee table. She was at the stage of drunk where she didn't care about anything, and manners were included in that list. "But don't worry. I'd already finished your order when I started on the wine." With a wave of her hand, she gestured to the large crate of products she'd left open on her worktable across the room. "One model of everything as you requested. I've been working on them day and night since last week."

Cecily investigated the devices. "These look perfect. Were they especially difficult?"

"Nope." The sofa seemed to be moving, and Astrid held on tightly to the armrest to keep from getting dizzy. "Easy."

After Cecily had examined each product and repacked it, she joined Astrid on the sofa. "Why the wine, Astrid?"

Astrid picked up her half-full glass from the table and swirled the liquid around, momentarily mesmerized by the way it traced the curved edges of the glass. "The World's Fair opens on Saturday. I'm celebrating for all those fine business-people who are setting up their booths tonight." She raised her glass and drained it. The wine had ceased to have a taste by now, becoming dull warmth that spread through her extremities, numbing any feelings that had begun to return. "I thought maybe I should get drunk, and then none of it would matter." She set the empty glass down on the table with a bit more force than was necessary. After a pause, she turned to Cecily, who was blurry around the edges. "So far, it still matters."

"Well, I have some good news." From her handbag, Cecily produced an envelope. "I have tickets to the private viewing of the Fair tomorrow night. Only open to business owners and those of us with connections. I thought you'd like to go."

Astrid stared at her, unsure if she was serious or not. Cecily had to know she wouldn't want to go. "That's nice, but I would rather..." She tried to think of a terrible alternative but, in her current state of mind, couldn't come up with anything clever. "I'd rather not. Thanks. I think I'm going to buy another bottle of wine and spend tomorrow like today."

"Going to the Fair will do you good. You can do some networking, perhaps."

"I don't give a *fuck* about networking right now." Astrid folded her arms, which took two tries. "And I don't want to go."

Cecily shook her head. "Astrid, I'm not going to let you waste away the best business opportunity in a decade by getting drunk in your flat. I want you to get out there and meet people and make some new contacts and get your mind off Eli." Her smile was firm. "Please, Astrid. As a favor to me. You owe me that much."

Astrid sighed. Cecily was right, and this wasn't worth fighting over. "Only if we don't go near Eli's booth. I don't want to see him."

"Of course." Cecily leaned over to pat her hand. "Please be sober tomorrow."

Astrid narrowed her eyes. "Fine."

28

As the train roared through the city, Astrid was plagued with an unpleasant sense of déjà vu. Less than a week earlier, she'd ridden this same train to the fairgrounds with Eli, excited and anxious about the judges' responses to their invention. That same night, she'd ridden it home alone. Now, here she was again, heading back to the fairgrounds, the sunset filling the train car with orange light.

From her handbag, she withdrew the ticket Cecily had given her the night before. She wanted to find the gold calligraphy pretentious, but it just made her jealous. If only Cecily were there to talk to her and take her mind off the situation, but she had a previous engagement and had promised to meet Astrid at the front gate. That left Astrid to ride the train alone, lost in her own thoughts. At least she'd recovered from her vicious hangover.

In the week since she'd been there, the fairgrounds had exploded into an immense display of color and light. After disembarking from the train, she stood staring up at the gates, her mouth open in awe despite how much she wanted to resent the Fair itself. She got caught up in the excitement of the crowd, much thinner than the opening-day crowds would be tomorrow but still thrumming with energy. An attendee punched her ticket at the main gate, and she stepped into the chaos of the World's Fair.

"Astrid!"

Cecily's voice made her turn. Her friend was pushing her way through a crowd, her face alight, and she pulled Astrid into a close hug. "I'm so glad you're here! I was worried you wouldn't come."

"Have you been waiting for me long?"

"No, only a few minutes. Isn't this incredible?" Cecily gestured to their surroundings.

"I've never seen anything like it." Astrid couldn't stop gaping. Downtown London was sad and deserted compared to this colorful showcase. "Where should we go first?"

Cecily took Astrid's arm and guided her down one aisle. "Let's start down here."

After a half hour of wandering from stall to stall, Astrid had almost forgotten she was supposed to be upset. Cecily had started her at the local business section, so the names on the shingles were familiar. These businessmen had set out their best wares, including many items she'd never seen before, so it was like seeing her favorite shops for the first time. Her emotions flickered between awe, amusement, fascination, and some unavoidable jealousy.

She was completely unprepared to turn away from a haberdashery and be facing the shingle for the Rutledge Emporium.

For a moment, she stood frozen, Cecily's hand tight on her arm keeping her rooted to the spot. Eli's booth was full of people, all gathered around him as he explained something to the enthralled onlookers. The sight of him burst a well of emotions inside her, and her throat closed up.

"Come on." Cecily tugged her forward.

"Cecily, I said I didn't want to be here. I was perfectly clear on that last night." Digging her heels into the dirt, Astrid tried to stay where she was. "Please."

"No. You need to see this." Cecily was larger and stronger than Astrid and easily dragged her into the booth.

The crowd parted enough so they could pass. When Astrid saw what they had been examining such intent, all the air rushed from her lungs.

Hanging above a large display table was a banner that read, "In partnership with Bailey's Felicitation Emporium." On the table, arrayed and showcased for everyone to see, were all her felicitation devices. At one side of the table, complete with its own display banner advertising its name and function, sat the Bailey-Rutledge Oscillating Felicitator. The Ossy.

Astrid stood motionless, her heart pounding hard enough to bruise her ribs. Eli hadn't seen her yet; he was engaged in animated conversation with a middle-aged woman who was filling out what appeared to be a mail-order form while she spoke. Astrid caught his voice above the crowd.

"That's right, ma'am. All work is guaranteed. Miss Bailey stands behind her brand. Felicitation devices ship in four to six weeks."

He was taking orders for her. He'd set up a display of her items, somehow, and he was selling her products. Her eyes prickled, and she pressed her lips together to steady her breathing so she didn't start to cry. Then Eli caught her gaze, and his conversation died midsentence.

The rest of the people in the booth seemed to dissolve in the intensity of his stare. Before she knew it, he was excusing himself from the conversation, passing through the crowd, and at last taking her hand to draw her away from everyone else.

It took Astrid a moment to find her voice. "How did you do all this?" She looked to where Cecily had taken up a position of authority behind the table, explaining the felicitation devices. "Where did you get the products?"

Eli took both her hands. She'd forgotten how good his hands felt in hers. "Cecily," he said. "It was all Cecily's idea. She came by my shop earlier this week and helped me set all of this up."

Of course. This was the delivery of products Cecily had picked up the night before. Everything was beginning to come together. "What about the judges? How can you get away with this?"

His eyes twinkled, his whole bearing radiating confidence. "There are no regulations about what products you can sell in your own booth, just what you can enter in the contest. Since I'm a 'reputable business,' I already have a booth, and they can't stop me from selling what I want. The IFCT wasn't happy about it, but there's nothing they can do."

"But...your business. Your reputation. What will the London Business Council say?"

Eli smiled. "I resigned from the council."

"You...resigned?" Astrid's head was swimming. "I don't understand. Last week, after the viewing, you left, and I thought...I thought..." Her voice trailed off.

Eli brought their entwined hands to his lips and kissed her knuckles. "I guess some things are more important than reputation. If I can help you build your business and get your shop, then it doesn't matter what some stodgy business owners think of me."

Astrid looked back to the crowd. Now that she had time to look properly, she recognized several familiar faces: the women from Tea and Talk had shown up, some with husbands in tow. There was Becky Peregol, Rowena, Sarah, Mildred, and even Edwina, with her mop of frizzy hair and high-collared dress. A rush of affection ran through her. Behind them all stood Josian. When Josian caught her eye, she took a step closer, but at the sight of her and Eli together, seemed to think better of it. She waved. They would catch up later.

"Your friends all came." Eli rubbed his thumb over the back of her hand. "I told Edwina, and she spread the word. Josian told me she came down as soon as she got your letter. Everyone's here for you. I had hoped Cecily could get you to show up."

The Tea and Talk members were only a handful of the two dozen or so people gathered in the booth, the overflow spilling out into the alleyway where they stood. "And all these people…they like the products?"

Eli nodded. "People have been placing orders all night. Between tonight and the next two weeks of the Fair, your earnings should be enough to get you started with your shop, I think."

Astrid tried to read the emotion in his eyes. "But why would you do all this?" She knew, but she needed him to say it; she needed to be absolutely sure.

He looked up at the sky above them, shaking his head and laughing. "Cecily's right. We are both the most stubborn people in the world." He cupped her cheek with his hand and looked into her eyes. "I did it because I love you. That scares the hell out of me, because I can't believe you really want to be with me, but I'm choosing to hope."

Astrid swallowed. "You don't care that I'm working class?"

Eli scoffed. "Of course not. That's not what had me hesitating. I've spent all this time thinking you could never want to be with me because I'm just another boring businessman."

Astrid laughed, the very idea absurd. "You're not boring! How could you ever think that you're boring?" She stepped in closer, speaking quieter so only he could hear. "Eli, you helped me make a fucking machine. And *test* it. That's not boring. That's the opposite of boring."

Eli smiled a small, secretive smile as he blushed. "I suppose I'm trying."

"I like that you're trying." Astrid slid her fingers into his hair. "I don't want you to think you aren't enough for me."

Eli slipped his arms around her waist. "I think we can make a go at this. If you want to. If you…if you feel the same."

Astrid smiled, her heart so full, it might burst. "Of course. I love you too, you prat."

Eli took her mouth under his and kissed the words right out of her. A few catcalls caught her attention, but she couldn't stop smiling against his lips.

29

The World's Fair preview wrapped up well after dark. Cecily had gone home already amid mutual well-wishes, and Josian had managed a few quick words to Astrid before promises that they would catch up soon. Astrid stayed to help Eli clean up before the grand opening of the Fair the next day. With the booth hangings locked closed and the fairgrounds nearly deserted, they boarded the last train back to town. Eli couldn't stop touching Astrid, wanting to reassure himself that she was really here beside him. In their empty train car, he drew her down onto his lap, and she turned her mouth to his.

Her kiss was chaste at first, an affectionate brush of the lips, but one touch and he needed more. He curled his hand in her hair and opened his mouth beneath hers. God, the feel of her, her taste, the quiet noises she made—he couldn't get enough.

Loud throat-clearing near him ended their intimate moment. The train conductor stood beside them, flushed with embarrassment and looking anywhere but at them as he held out his hand for their tickets. Astrid giggled into Eli's neck as he handed them over. When the conductor punched their tickets and left, trotting away in haste, she pressed another openmouthed kiss to Eli's neck.

He buried his face in her hair. The anxiety, the sacrifices, the most stressful week of his life, all of it had paid off. He was still a little uncertain of the future, but he could live with that uncertainty. He could learn to trust.

As if reading his mind, Astrid murmured the question in his ear. "So you think I'm worth all this headache?"

Eli leaned back and brushed a lock of her hair out of her eyes, tucking it behind her ear. It slipped out again, making them both smile. "Are you kidding? A lifetime of Gowen Woodbridge and the London Business Council versus a lifetime of you? No contest."

She dropped another kiss on his lips, her mouth curved in a teasing smile. "I don't know if I'm ready for a lifetime. You're kind of an arse."

"Like attracts like, doesn't it?"

When she opened her mouth to object, he swallowed her protests, kissing her slowly, thoroughly, exploring her mouth as though he had a lifetime to kiss her. And he did, didn't he?

When he had to come up for air, head spinning, he rested his forehead against hers. In the dark train car, her face was illuminated only sporadically by the lights of the passing city buildings. They would reach their stop soon.

He asked the question into her lips. "Your flat or mine?"

"Mine."

Fog had rolled in by the time they disembarked in the center of the city. The walk back to her flat was dreamlike. In the thick haze, broken only by the amber glow of streetlights, they passed through the city like shadows. When he looked back on this walk, he would remember little. Her warm hand in his was the only solid thing in the world, their walk punctuated by kisses between the orange halos of light.

In her flat, though, she dragged him into her arms and everything became real again. His need for her was so urgent, he thought it might tear him apart, but he simultaneously wanted to take things slowly, to memorize every inch of her skin. She dragged him into the bedroom, her hands on the lapels of his waistcoat, pulling him on top of her as she fell back onto the bed.

Eli broke the kiss to catch his breath, his heart racing as he sat back on his heels. They were both fully clothed. "Do you want to slow down?"

Astrid tugged at his jacket, pushing it off his shoulders. "No. I want you naked."

Her urgency was hard to resist. He let her undress him, working through the buttons on his vest and shirt. She brushed against his erection, first by accident, then deliberately, tracing his length through his trousers. Her touch sent shivers through his skin, and his need moved from urgent to desperate.

Why did women wear so many layers of clothing? When he fumbled with the hook-and-eye closures of her corset, she took mercy on him and unfastened it herself. After more pulling and tugging and endless rows of buttons, they were both finally undressed.

Her body was glorious; he felt as if he were seeing her for the first time, all cream-colored skin with dusky-brown nipples he had to suck. She threaded her fingers in his hair, her nails scratching the back of his head as he moved from one breast to the other. It wasn't enough. He wanted her crying out beneath his hands and tongue. He kissed his way down her stomach and spread her legs.

It only took one slow, thorough swipe of his tongue to make her arch up off the bed with a wordless cry. He loved that sound. When he did it again, she moaned. He took her clit between his lips and listened as her cries became louder, less restrained, her hips beginning to writhe beneath his ministrations. It was about all he could take; he wanted to bury himself inside her, feel her shuddering around him, her muscles milking his cock. He slid two fingers inside her tight, wet sheath and pressed upward.

"Fuck! Oh, *fuck.*"

He loved the way she swore when she was close. A bit more and she would come on his fingers. He could pull back now, make her wait, but he wanted to bring her that release. Rather than drawing back, he continued sucking her clit, even catching it gently between his teeth as he added a third finger.

She came with a keening cry, her hips arching, then reflexively pulled back as the pleasure became overwhelming. He held her in place with one hand on her hip, driving her through the waves as he kept sucking her sensitive bud. Her fingernails dug painfully into his scalp as she shivered through the aftershocks.

Astrid collapsed, spent, glistening with perspiration. Eli waited, a little smug at the sight of her trying to catch her breath. At last she smiled, reaching up to pull his lips to hers, probably tasting herself in his mouth, and a moment later he felt her fingers wrap around his dick. His arms buckled, and he buried his face in her neck.

Each stroke of her hand sent a shiver down his spine. She

rubbed over the slick head of his cock, making him moan. She needed to stop, needed to give him a moment to recover, or this would be over too soon. He brushed her hand away and sat back on his heels.

Leaning past him, she opened her nightstand drawer. Her pessary box lay in the back, nestled amid a collection of felicitation devices. She took out the box and slid her pessary inside herself, and he watched her finger disappear, wanting nothing more than to bury his cock right there. When she went to put the box back, though, she paused, looking at something in the pile. She sat up with a brass device in her hand and gave Eli a devious smile.

"Do you know what this is?"

He took it from her to study. From a narrow tip, the shaft widened gradually down its length then narrowed sharply before a flared base. He wanted to shake his head no, but the smile on her face gave him an idea about the device's purpose. His mouth went dry, pulse beginning to race. He gave a half shrug.

Astrid knelt up on the bed, taking his face between her hands. She kissed him, her mouth warm and soft, putting one hand on his chest. Surely she could feel how fast his heart was beating.

She asked her question against his mouth. "Will you let me fuck you with this?"

Eli's cock stiffened even more, somehow, as his face heated with a blush. Astrid's hand moved from his chest to his erection, wrapping around the thick shaft and squeezing. His eyes fluttered closed, and it became difficult to think. As she worked his cock, she kissed him again, and his hand tightened on the device he was still holding. He wanted to know what it felt like.

Astrid drew back again, her hand still wrapped around his length. "Well?"

He nodded.

"Hmm? I didn't hear you." Astrid took the product from him, smiling. "What was that?"

He pushed her onto the bed and climbed over her, wanting to kiss away that smug smirk even while he held back the urge to part her legs and plunge inside her. "Yes," he said against her lips. "Yes, I want you to fuck me."

With both hands on his chest, she rolled him onto his back. His erection bobbed against his stomach, and his pulse thundered in his ears. Astrid took a jar off the nightstand then sat between his legs, forcing them apart. She was actually going to do this. He couldn't help but watch as she dipped her finger in the jar. She rubbed against his hole, dipping in and around him, the feeling making him grip the bedsheets with both hands. She probed with her finger before the cold brass brushed against him.

Astrid moved the shaft slowly at first, pressing inward, and Eli's cock stiffened impossibly at the sensation. This shouldn't feel so good, but it did. Inch by inch, she slid it inside. The device had seemed small in his hand, but like this, it seemed to go on forever. Then, it rubbed against a spot inside him that made him buck up off the bed. Holy hell, that stole his breath. Astrid began moving the shaft back out again, just as slowly. When only the tip remained inside, she pushed it in once more, hitting that same place. In and out, in and out, she was fucking him, and the motions had him burning up from the inside.

"Fuck, Astrid. Oh my *God*." He couldn't stop babbling. He wanted her to stop, wanted her to continue, couldn't think and couldn't form a coherent sentence. His cock was dripping against his stomach, and if she did so much as touch him, he would explode.

"Does it feel good when I fuck you?" Her voice was throaty and low, and just the sound of it was almost enough to send him over the edge.

Eli groaned, not sure if he could answer, and she sped up. "I'm going to make you come," she said. "And I want you to watch me do it."

He managed to open his eyes. The sight of Astrid sitting between his legs, that wicked expression on her face, made him shiver. He was so close. Each time she thrust that shaft inside, she brushed the spot that seemed directly connected to his cock so that he was painfully close to a climax without any contact at all. It wasn't enough, though. He needed her touch.

Past the point of caring, he wanted her so badly, wanted this orgasm that hovered right out of reach. "Please touch me," he begged.

Astrid smiled, continuing to fuck him over and over again before finally reaching out to grasp his cock with her other hand.

He came immediately, his orgasm exploding from somewhere deep inside him, the fullness driving him over the top. Maybe he was crying out, maybe he was moaning, but he couldn't focus on anything but the spiraling, gut-clenching pleasure. As he began to come down, she pushed the brass plug a bit farther, and his hole closed around the narrow part of the shaft, holding it in place with the flared base outside. He shivered, the aftershocks of his orgasm making him clench around this plug still filling him up. With a soft cloth, she cleaned up the mess from his stomach and leaned down to kiss him.

"Christ, Astrid, that was amazing." He brushed his hand across her cheek, and she smiled.

"Thank you."

Shifting slightly made the plug shift inside him as well. In the aftermath of his climax, it felt strange. "Are you forgetting something?"

Astrid raised an eyebrow. "I hope you don't think we're done here."

A tremor ran through him as she moved down his body again. Without any hesitation, she took his softening cock in her mouth.

He was not ready for that, the rush of feeling sharp enough to border on pain. She took her time, laving his tip with her tongue, waiting for him to catch up. He was too sensitive, each touch making him twitch, but he soon began to stiffen in her mouth regardless. As he became more aroused, she pushed on the base of the plug again, making him hard in no time at all. His cock was still tender, but he wanted more. God, he loved this woman. Eli pulled Astrid up to his mouth and rolled her over, plunging inside her with one long stroke.

The first thrust was all velvety warmth and unbearable tightness. She gasped at the full length of him, her fingernails biting into the skin of his back as he settled into the cradle of her hips. He held still for a moment, relishing being inside her, until she began to squirm beneath him. Her impatience made him smile; even with the plug inside him, the urgency of his first orgasm was gone. "Easy. There's no rush." Holding himself in check, he slowly withdrew then thrust again, and again, setting up a steady rhythm.

Her eyes fell closed, back arching, the long column of her neck exposed. He bent down to suck and bite the tender skin there, needing to taste her again. She writhed beneath him, her pussy clenching once around his cock, and he paused at the sudden sensation threatening to overwhelm him. Rolling slightly to one side, he worked one hand between them.

As soon as he brushed her swollen bud, Astrid's mouth fell open. He bit his lip, focusing all his concentration on her pleasure, willing himself to hold out even as each thrust moved the plug perfectly inside him. When she curled her legs up and wrapped them over his hips, he sunk even deeper inside her wet heat. The urge was too great; he couldn't stop thrusting harder and harder, moving her back and forth on the bed with each stroke. She was close, her skin flushing beautifully red across her neck and chest.

"Look at me," he said.

She opened her eyes, large and luminous in the dim light. His gaze locked on hers. "Don't look away."

Her eyes widened briefly, muscles fluttering again. Oh, so she liked that. He wanted to drive her out of herself, wanted to watch her in this most beautiful and vulnerable moment as she succumbed to release. His thumb pressed insistent circles on her bud until she started to clench around him and then, all at once, fell over the edge. Her entire body stiffened, and she clung fiercely to him, her eyelids fluttering as she struggled to keep them open as he had asked. She curled up into him, pressing her breasts into his chest. Her pussy contracted in rolling spasms, squeezing his cock so tightly, it took his breath away. That was all he needed to tumble over too, euphoria tearing through him as he erupted inside her. He closed his eyes and collapsed, the aftershocks rushing through him in shivering waves.

Finally, Eli regained thought and rolled off of her. He took care of the plug, still trembling, and then rejoined her on the bed where she held out her arms to him. Eli went willingly. She was going to be the death of him. Cupping his cheek with her hand, Astrid brushed her thumb across his lips. "I love you."

Hearing her say it like this, no pretense, no jokes, made his heart swell. "I love you too." He kissed her fingers.

Astrid rested both arms behind her head. "You're still kind of an arse sometimes."

Eli couldn't help but laugh. "Maybe I am. Do you still want me?"

She shrugged. "I suppose I can get used to it. Might take a while, though. Maybe a lifetime."

Rolling over, he gathered her into his arms. "I think we have that long."

ACKNOWLEDGMENTS

Revisiting *Combustion* after so many years away has been a delight. I'm happy to have been able to update the book to my current standards, including what I hope is clearer consent, steamier sex, and all-around stronger writing. The narrative itself is unchanged, and that's mostly due to the amazing developmental editing skills of Christa Desir way back when this book was first published. For this edition, I was able to work with Manu Velasco for copy edits, and their attention to detail helped this book shine. My cover is all thanks to the amazing Erin Dameron-Hill of EDHProfessionals, who creates gorgeous art and was a delight to work with. As always, I'm immeasurably grateful for my agent Saritza Hernandez for supporting me in developing a multifaceted writing career.

Creating art of any kind in a global pandemic is a challenging and humbling endeavor. I have relied more than ever on the kindness of my social circle: my husband and co-conspirator Chris, Crystal the beloved couch goblin, my bestie and sounding board Laura, Amanda the desert-dwelling cheerleader, and everyone on the Liscord. I would have loved to do these edits over pastry and coffee with Ray, but I'm hopeful for more of that in the future.

Combustion was a book ahead of its time when it was first published back in 2015, and I am grateful for the opportunity to update and rerelease it now. Most of all, I appreciate you, the reader, for taking a chance on Astrid and Eli and their scandalous World's Fair adventure.

ABOUT THE AUTHOR

RITA™ Award-winning author Elia Winters is a fat, tattooed, polyamorous bisexual who loves petting cats and fighting the patriarchy. She holds a Master's degree in English Literature and teaches at a small rural high school, where she also runs the drama club. In her spare time, she is equally likely to be found playing tabletop games, kneading bread, cross-stitching, or binge-watching Marie Kondo. A sex educator and kink-positive feminist, Elia reviews sex toys, speaks at kink conventions, and writes geeky, kinky, cozy erotic romance. She currently lives in western Massachusetts with her loving husband and their weird pets.

ALSO BY ELIA WINTERS

Comes In Threes

Three-Way Split

Just Past Two

Three For All

Slices of Pi

Even Odds

Tied Score

Single Player

Stand-Alone Titles

Purely Professional

Playing Knotty

Hairpin Curves

Stay informed about Elia Winters! Receive bonus content and subscriber-only specials, plus info on new releases and personal appearances.

eliawinters.com/newsletter